NEW MEXICO STORIES

TOLD BY CHILE CHARLIE

First edition August 2021

Design Cover by a KDP

ISBN: 9798878329989

ACKNOWLEDGEMENTS

Thanks to my colleagues and editors for encouraging me to create these stories and my fictitious character, Chile Charlie. He has become a pillar of strength in my writing life.

Thanks also to the dozens of contributive thoughts, experiences, and research to do this book. Jack Barclay, Austin Jones, and Lindsey Jones were among the most helpful and supportive.

On a personal note, a huge thanks to my wife, Jean Natalie Pintar, for bearing with me during the writing phase of this project; she was a total rock star, always supporting and encouraging me.

I want to shout out to my caregiver, Mary Holguin, as she took care of my invalid wife while I spent many hours in front of the computer, unable to provide the caregiving services that a husband should do.

TABLE OF CONTENTS

INTRODUCTION

Throughout the evolution of language, individuals have found joy in immersing themselves in fictional journeys and experiences of imaginary characters. This practice alleviates monotony and makes the hours pass quicker and more enjoyable.

There is no need for further endorsement. The primary purpose and rationale for engaging in this unique collection of stories is pursuing pleasure and knowledge. These stories are crafted to brighten your day and serve as a delightful escape.

Modern fiction writers are artistically more self-conscious than I am. I realize there are many ways of telling a story; I decided upon a method before writing and even setting up rules. Instead of telling the story myself, I would let my character, Chile Charlie, tell it through interviews or secondhand information. I confine myself to the recordings of the thoughts of my character.

▲ ▲ ▲

Chile Charlie and Doug Salazar stood on the back porch of Doug's cabin, a rustic retreat to accommodate six hunting elk enthusiasts. While not the most architecturally sound, the cabin offered protection from the elements with its cedar planks on the exterior. The cedar planks provided durability and made the cabin energy-efficient by resisting insects and rot while offering excellent insulation.

The inside had a stove, and rustic furniture adorned the space, complemented by three homemade bunk beds.

"Doug, your cabin is perfect for a weekend getaway. Do you get many clients?"

"Yes, we are always busy during the elk season and have fewer bookings the rest of the year."

"It's not like in the 1850s when New Mexico was a territory," Charlie said.

"Why did it take so long for New Mexico to reach statehood, Doug?"

Doug, an enthusiastic community leader, looked up with a puzzled expression. "Ah, the statehood question. It's a complicated tale, my friend. Let's unravel this story."

Charlie sat, eager to hear and understand the problems involved.

"I can't wrap my head around the problem. New Mexico was a vital part of the Old West for many years. It was still not part of the United States until the early 20th century, on January 6, 2012.

"You see, Chile Charlie, it's a blend of politics, historical baggage, and public sentiment. The issues were always entangled in the web of complex factors."

"Break it down for me, Doug; I need to know."

Doug leaned back and took a sip of his hot coffee. "First, there is the political game. Over the years, different parties had quite different views on statehood. Some feared a change in status would upset the balance of power and did not want to take that risk.

Charlie nods. "Politics as always."

"Then there's the historical aspect. New Mexico's history dates back to the 19th century. Generations have grown up under the status quo, and change was met with resistance."

Charlie tapped his finger, "So it's like breaking with tradition."

"Exactly." And don't forget the economic concerns of the railroads and mining industries.

Some worlds face financial and political challenges with a change," Doug said.

Scratching his head, Charlie said, "But shouldn't the benefits have outweighed the challenges?"

Doug said, "In theory, yes. But perceptions can be hard to change. There are the issues of power and cultural identity."

Charlie sighs, "It seems like New Mexico was caught in a never-ending loop of problems and issues."

Doug provided a list of the rejections that needed to be overcome:

1. Southern members of Congress objected to the anti-slavery provision of the document.

2. The mining and railroad industries oppose preferring territorial status with its lack of state taxation.

3. The costly Native American wars created a negative image dominated by the primitive population.

4. Wild West image of lawlessness, irresponsibility, and violence perpetuated by Billy the Kid and other outlaws.

5. New Mexico's economy depended on agriculture, mining, and ranching. That did not match the interest of the eastern states.

Doug said, "Change is always met with resistance, my friend. But progress takes time. The tide of changes and New Mexico's statehood became a reality on January 6, 1912, with the right political climate and public sentiments aligning themselves."

CHAPTER ONE

ARRIVAL

He was about to get sidetracked.

Prairie Grass Pete was in a predicament when he brought Illinois Chile peppers into New Mexico and attempted to sell them. His motivation was fueled by the need for funds for gas for the remainder of his trip to Las Cruces. However, he encountered a significant hurdle. The New Mexico Legislature had enacted a law prohibiting the sale of Chile peppers grown outside the state. Compounding his troubles, Prairie Grass Pete found himself confined to the Clovis City Jail due to the regrettable mistake he made.

He sat in the Clovis City Jail for two months. Finally, the local district attorney decided to let Prairie Grass Pete go. But he had three conditions before being released. One, he had to change his appearance; two, he had to change his mode of transportation; and three, he had to change his purpose of traveling to New Mexico.

Prairie Grass Pete changed his Midwest attire, mode of transportation, and name. He changed into

7

chaps, boots, and a T-shirt with Great American Duck Races on the back. He would get a giant sombrero to top off his attire and become Chile Charlie.

He sold his John Deere tractor and found an old Ford El Camino pickup truck. The El Camino was a 1959 version and had rusted fenders. He swapped with no additional money. You might wonder why he gave up his tractor for a pickup truck. He reasoned that the distance between communities in New Mexico was so great that it would take him too long to travel from one community to another on a tractor. So, the faster transportation would be a pickup truck-- especially in El Camino truck was his reasoning.

The third thing he had to do was change his purpose. In Illinois, he aimed to gather information about communities and hold talks at public schools. His new objective would be to create storybooks for children and adults about the history of small New Mexican towns.

Now you have this story about why Prairie Grass Pete has not reported his progress for the last several months. His new destination is Portales, New Mexico. He hoped to get there soon if the El Camino would hold together until he arrived.

CHAPTER TWO

WHAT IS IN A NAME?

Seated in his newly acquired El Camino, Chile Charlie left Clovis and drove with great dispatch to the campus town of Portales, New Mexico. On the way, he knew how straight and unyielding the road was. He looked to the right and saw vast nothingness. He glanced to the left and saw vast nothingness. The only thing he saw on the trip were small rabbit-like moles crossing the highway before him.

Chile Charlie was used to hours of boredom interspersed with moments of stark fear on his travels from Illinois. This loneliness was nothing to be concerned about, he thought. He was so looking forward to his arrival in Portales. The time he passed was much like molasses in December in Vermont. He finally arrived after his sixty-minute solitary ride.

Chile Charlie eyed his surroundings as he entered the northeast corner of Portales, New Mexico, the home of Eastern New Mexico University. He was anxious as a frog on a log waiting for his supper to talk to somebody about the city.

He spotted a young student who he surmised would be a good person to start a dialogue. She wore a white see-through blouse, washed-out jeans, and western alligator boots. Her hair was chopped short, giving her the look of a 1950 page-style haircut cut. Her face showed the signs of New Mexico's 365 days of sunshine. She looked like she had been toasted in a super quick toaster.

Chile Charlie introduced himself and asked the young lady for her name. She said, "My name is Dora Dominguez-Garcia-Espina-Dickerson-O'Rieely. People called me Dora for short."

Chile Charlie was filled with questions he wanted to ask, but the most critical question was how Portales got its name.

Here is the story that young Dora told him of how the city got its name. "The city was named for a nearby campsite where spring waters gushed from caves resembling porches. Thus--Portales are porches in Spanish. Portales Springs was the most famous watering hole on the Old Fort Sumner Trail. It hosted Comanche, Indians, buffalo hunters, ranchers, and Billy the Kid."

Portales is on the eastern border of the state. Portales is New Mexico's front door to the east of

New Mexico. Portales fits the description of a friendly university town even more today than when it was coined in the 1800s. *Wow*, thought, Chile Charlie, what an exciting story.

Chile Charlie camped out in Portales for a few days to discover other stories about the area, especially the university.

As he tried to sleep, he was struck by the sky. It was filled with thousands of white dots. The moon was directly overhead. It gave a wonderful glow that made Chile Charlie think back to when the American team of astronauts landed on the moon many years ago.

Chile Charlie continues his exploration of Portales. "Gee Whiz," said Chile Charlie to himself. I must acquire more evidence about this spot in the road named for "porches."

After a good night's snooze on a park bench, he began his quest for an "intelligent--know it all person" to fill him in about the college, peanuts, cows, and flyboys in Portales.

Chile Charlie did his best imitation of Jane Fonda's exercise, stretching to the fore until all his body parts were placed correctly. He stepped out smartly like a GI on a mission to capture someone who could give him a good Eastern New Mexico University narrative. He stopped at the corner coffee shop, sat down, and started a set of rapid-fire questions to a distinguished local named Christopher Humberblank. Chris wore traditional going-to-class apparel---Cargo Shorts, a Nike Polo shirt, and open-faced sandals. He told Chile Charlie that the university was a four-year institution with branches in Roswell and Ruidoso and that he liked his technology major.

Chile Charlie gave the university the nickname Harvard of New Mexico because of the Ivy League look of the buildings. Chris laughed but agreed that was a good observation.

Next, Chile Charlie asked Chris what made Portales's economy hum. He thought for a while, then answered, "Nuts, heifers, and flyboys."

Chris continued to elaborate. Portales has the most extensive organic peanut acreages next to the state of Georgia. There is a vast dairy industry that produces beef cattle and cheese. Cannon Air Force Base is only a stone's throw away from Portales. Many families live and shop in the City of Porches.

Chile Charles conveyed his gratitude to Chris. With the belief that he possessed sufficient information about Portales, Charlie decided to proceed to Roswell, which was sixty miles away.

CHAPTER THREE

ALIEN CITY USA

As Chile Charlie drove for about half an hour, he turned on his radio. The first station was a news station. He was not up to the news, so he got a new station that featured country-western music. He was taken by the new song he hadn't heard before as he drove sixty miles an hour. Bobby Bare sang Jesus Kicked My Ass through the Goal Post of Life. Chile Charlie thought that the song reminded him of his life.

Chile Charlie arrived in Roswell at 6:45 PM. He got there just in time to observe God's magic of a beautiful and incredible sunset that can only be seen in the great state of New Mexico. God had outdone himself this time.

Charlie had conjured up beautiful gold-attended clouds surrounded by spears of light purple. The topography of Roswell is tabletop flat. You could see the sunset as the sun ducks below the horizon.

Chile Charlie carved out the mission to find a space alien. He strolled down Main Street, looking for one of the bug-eyed aliens that permeated the city. He came across this strange-looking person, Mr. Bill Azinger.

Chile Charlie deduced rapidly that Bill was not an alien. He was very tall; he looked like a man who had played basketball for a college team. He had crew-cut hair, a clean-shaven tanned face, blue jeans with crocodile boots, and the most excellent-looking pair of blue eyes one would ever want to see. Chile Charlie went to work on Bill Azinger, asking about this Rowell alien story. Bill asked Chile Charlie to sit on the park bench to get comfortable to hear the Roswell aliens' story.

The story is; "In mid-1947, a military Air Force surveillance balloon crashed, prompting claims alleging the crash was of an extraterrestrial spaceship. After an initial spike of interest, the military reported that the crash was merely a conventional weather balloon.

"Interest subsequently waned until the late 1970s. Ufologists began promulgating a variety of increasingly elaborate conspiracy theories. They claimed that one or more alien spacecraft had crash-landed and that the extraterrestrial occupants had been recovered.

"In the 1990s, the US military published reports disclosing the true nature of the crashed Project Mogul balloon. Nevertheless, the Roswell incident continues to interest those in the popular media. Roswell has been reported as "the world's most famous, most exhaustively investigated, and most debunked UFO claim.

"Now, that's our story, and we are sticking to it. We will use it as best possible to attract as many visitors to Roswell as possible."

Chile Charlie decided that he had enough information about the alien issue of Roswell and wanted to skedaddle. He will try to make it to Las

Cruces tonight. Satisfied with the story, Chile Charlie mounted his El Camino and headed out.

He gave thanks to Bill Azinger. He then asked for directions to get out of town and go to Las Cruces.

His El Camino was full of gas and had all cylinders working, so he put the pedal to the metal and headed out. He may come back to Roswell. It was an enjoyable ride through the Hondo Valley. On each side of the road, he could see evidence of the history of Billy the Kid, Pat Garrett, and other gunfighters of long ago.

CHAPTER FOUR

TRAVELING DAYDREAMS

As Chile Charlie passed through Hondo Valley, he saw the small school district buildings and wondered how the students could get a broad view of the world when they became adult citizens. The thoughts left his mind as fast as they came in.

He continued driving until he arrived in the small town of Ruidoso. Stopping to take a break, Charlie found Henry Winkler. He was a small, weather-worn, longtime village resident. Charlie engaged Henry, with a face ready to smile and a disposition to match, in a conversation about what makes Ruidoso prosper. Charlie started the discussion with the question, why would anybody want to visit Ruidoso? Henry's response was concise and to the point. "People come to Ruidoso to escape the hubbub of city life or the boredom of country life."

People have said the village is the ultimate Playground of the Southwest. It is a village that has accepted the unusual. Art galleries are everywhere, and artists are creative with their pottery, paintings, and carvings. Ruidoso has a thriving tourist industry with two casinos, world-class horseracing—Home of the American Fortuity for quarter horses, entertainment, and seasonal recreation at Ski Apache.

Chile Charlie told Henry Winkler that his noggin was filled with the sugar plums of Ruidoso, and he had to be on his way to get to Las Cruces before dark. Chile Charlie said goodbye to Henry Azinger.

Charlie got into his El Camino, started the engine, revved it to total capacity, and headed up the mountain to rendezvous with his good friends in Las Cruces.

He was concerned that his El Camino might have difficulty climbing the steep grade. He drove up the mountain to 7500 feet. The engine started to overheat. He pulled over to the side of the road to give the engine a short rest. The engine cooled off enough for him to start the rapid descent to Mescalero. It didn't take Charlie long till he was at the outskirts of the headquarters for the Mescalero Indian Tribe.

His only concern was time. He wanted to visit the Mescalero Museum. He had heard many remarkable things about this little museum and wanted to see its contents. So, he pulled off the main highway and entered the business section of the city of Mescalero.

He quickly found the museum. As he entered the facility, a charming female volunteer guide met Chile Charlie. Her name was Red Rope Runner. She was short, stocky, and wore a traditional Mescalero dress. Red Rope Runner was a very engaging young lady willing to answer all Chile Charlie's questions. He studied the history of the Mescalero Tribe and their present situation. After about forty-five minutes, he said his goodbyes to Red Rope Runner, got back into his vehicle, and continued his descent to Tularosa.

He could see the outlines of White Sands National Park fifty miles away. The air was clean and fresh, and he was pleasantly surprised by the vastness of the White Sands area.

Chile Charlie was hurrying to get to Las Cruces, so he spent little time in Tularosa. He found a couple of interesting sites. One was a seminary for the Catholic Church. And the second was a small rug store. He stopped at the rug store to see if he could find an unusual, original New Mexican-crafted rug. Charlie was disappointed when he discovered that all rugs were commercially manufactured in China. He returned to his El Camino and headed for Alamogordo, fourteen miles away.

He wanted to stop at the New Mexico Museum of Space History quickly. He got out his GPS and headed directly for the Space History Museum. He was satisfied with what he found there.

He saw space paraphernalia worn by the early astronauts, history, and early space travel pictures. Chile Charlie couldn't stay long because he wanted to make Las Cruces before nightfall. Las Cruces was eighty miles away, and he had to pass through the White Sands Missile Range and climb another mountain of 6500 feet before descending into Las Cruces.

After his long, hair-rising, and beautiful travels Chile Charlie finally made his destination: Las Cruces. New stories about towns and villages in the southwest could be in the making. It's been a long journey for him, but he is ready to discover the history and culture that the Old West Country would provide.

Charlie spent a few days meditating after his arduous trip from Illinois to Las Cruces, Chile. Where was he going to finish this respite time?

He looked around to find a quiet place. He could go to one of the many public parks and sleep under the stars. But he had been sleeping under the stars for some time. So, he took refuge in the Gospel Mission in the central section of Las Cruces. You see, Chile Charlie was not financially well off with no spending money to waste. However, he also wanted to talk to some local characters about what they like about Las Cruces and the southwest corner of New Mexico.

CHAPTER FIVE

BEGINNING OF A NEW LIFE

The following day, Chile Charlie stepped briskly out on the veranda where he met Alvin Hawkpa, who looked like he might have been a longtime resident of Las Cruces. Alvin was tall and slender with delicate bird-like bones. His hands were smooth, the skin transparent enough for the small blue veins to show through.

As they sat on the veranda, Hawkpa said, I'm fifty-four years old."

Charlie thought he was too young for the massiveness of weight that characterizes older men at the Mission.

Chile Charlie told himself; *I will start a conversation with Alvin and discover what Las Cruces and the surrounding area offer.*

Charlie's first question to Alvin was, "How long have you lived in Dona Ana County?"

Alvin said, "Except for two years in the Navy, all my life!"

"Great, then you can be my guide to places to visit and people to interview," Chile Charlie said.

Alvin rattled off things he thought visitors wanted to learn about the area. Charlie should visit Santa Teresa and the Union Pacific intermodal railyards at the southern portion of Dona Ana County and progress north. It is Dona Ana's newest Economic Development activity.

"Oh! Chile Charlie, you don't want to miss Sunland Park's Horseracing Track. It is one of the best in the country and has been the home of several Derby winners. Other must-see landmarks are the dairy farms that are adjacent to Interstate 10. You can smell them three miles away. You can't miss them; follow your nose," uttered Alvin.

"A great site to see is the Stahmann's Pecan Farms. The Stahmann family owns the largest pecan farm in New Mexico and produces most of the exported pecans worldwide. It would take you several days to enjoy the relaxation of the pecan orchards.

"You don't want to miss the quaint little Town of Mesilla. It is one of the towns that claim Billy the Kid was jailed. The Plaza is the center of cultural life, with many festivals and outdoor events held annually," Mr. Hawkpa exclaimed.

"Then, of course, there is Las Cruces itself. The second-largest city in New Mexico and the home of New Mexico's State University, famed for its aeronautical engineering department and basketball teams. You would not want to miss the Downtown Farmers Market, which is open year-round on Wednesday and Saturday mornings. Other attractions you want to see are the New Mexico Farm and Ranch Museum, the numerous art galleries that punctuate the downtown area, the Railroad Museum, and the Veteran's Memorial Park."

"Chile Charlie, when you leave Las Cruces and travel north on Interstate 10, you find the small villages of Radium Springs, Rincon, and Hatch. These have no industry. People who want to live in small communities find these towns very enticing," Alvin Hawkpa said.

Alvin said, "Chile Charlie, I am getting a little chilled and must stop at this point in my pinpoint traveler's guide and continue to talk about each of the places next time we meet."

CHAPTER SIX

CHILE CHARLIE DISCOVERS THE PREHISTORIC TRACKWAYS NATIONAL MONUMENT

Chile Charlie decided the weather was enticing to be outdoors and visited the Prehistoric Trackways National Monument northwest of Las Cruces. During this trip, He was told he could get a glimpse of Dona Ana County's history and beauty.

Charlie jumped into his El Camino and headed out. He traveled the asphalt, gravel, and sand roads to find the exact location of the Prehistoric Trackways National Monument. It took forty-five minutes to reach the entranceway to the national monument.

The monument contains the fossilized footprints of amphibians, reptiles, and even some previously unknown insects dating back 280 million years before dinosaurs. What a national treasure this must be, Chile Charlie thought.

Chile Charlie looked around for a human to give him some background about the Prehistoric Trackways National Monument. He found Henie Armijo, a fella who resembled the original desert rat. He looked like he spent too much time under a powerful sun lamp and walked waist-deep in molasses.

Mr. Armijo told Chile Charlie about the Monument. "Back in the 1980s, a citizen paleontologist, Jerry MacDonald, stumbled upon the thousands of trackways in the Robledo Mountains.

"Under the supervision of the Smithsonian Natural History Museum and the Carnegie Museum, McDonald helped excavate more than 2500 slabs of fossilized records. This area is known as the discovery site. There are detailed markings of plants, petrified wood, amphibians, and reptiles. Most slabs can now be found in the Jerry MacDonald Paleozoic Trackways collection at the New Mexico Museum of Natural History and Sciences in Albuquerque. Still, several can also be seen at the Las Cruces Museum of Nature and Science."

Henie moved to a shelter to get out of the sun. He resumed, "Created in March 2009, the area was designated a National Monument. Individuals wanted to preserve the integrity of future excavations due to being major deposits of the Paleozoic Era and containing one of the most scientifically significant Early Permian track sites."

Mr. Armijo explained to Chile Charlie, "These unique fossils are unlike anything ever discovered in the country and even globally. These trackways serve as a Rosetta Stone, enabling the interpretation and understanding of ancient fossils worldwide."

Then Mr. Armijo declared, "For the more interested in the current ecosystem, the Monument is a fitting example of the Chihuahuan desert. With its flora of grama grass, agave, yucca, barrel cactus, button cactus, Scheer's pincushion cactus, claret cup cactus, prickly pear, ocotillo acacia, and honey mesquite."

As the conversation continued, Chile Charlie discovered that other draws to the area beyond the educational opportunities include hiking, horseback riding, bike trails with a challenging five-and-a-half-mile route, and even a chance to evaluate all-terrain vehicles. There are thirty-two miles of designated off-highway vehicle routes; half require modified vehicles and special driving skills.

Chile Charlie headed into a canyon. He spent about five hours exploring the Prehistoric Trackway's National Monument. It was worth every minute. Charlie thought that others should join him in discovering this jewel.

Chile Charlie discovered that Dona Anna County has nationally notable features for paleontologists, scientists, educators, and those who want to see the scenery.

CHAPTER SEVEN

CHILE CHARLIE EXPLORES SPACEPORT AMERICA

Spaceport America is a must-see attraction for Chile Charlie today. He has read and heard so much about this outstanding attraction that he made the sixty-mile trip north of Las Cruces. Chile Charlie went to the local filling station to ensure enough gas for the journey. The filling station was the local 7-Eleven convenience store. He gathered chips, peanuts, and a large drink to keep him company on his hour-long trip.

He navigated his way to Interstate 25 North. When he got on the Interstate, he put the pedal to the metal to the outstanding speed of sixty-five mph. As he looked out the window, he saw the fenders of his El Camino doing a version of a pelican on its quest to feed itself. The fenders were flapping fast and furious. It made the El Camino want to fly.

The trip from Las Cruces to Spaceport America took an hour and thirty minutes because the last few miles to the facility were an unpaved, bumpy dirt road-- not very futuristic. There is a two-headed discussion about paving the entrance road to the facility. One option is to request money from the New Mexico state legislature, a long shot, or use some of the existing tax revenues from the two participating counties. As usual, there is a drumbeat for each side. Yet there still is an unpaved, bumpy dirt road.

After the bone-jarring trip on the dirt road, Chile Charlie's jawbone dropped at least an inch. Before him stood a futuristic-looking building that contained the headquarters for Spaceport America.

The building was a vast, out-of-place-looking facility. Chile Charlie looked around for a place to park his less-than-futuristic-looking El Camino.

He must've looked out of place when Donald Straight found him wandering around the building, looking for a door to enter the facility. Mr. Straight was a trim-looking six-foot-three-inch specimen of a man. Donald wore regular blue jeans and a polo shirt with a Spaceport America logo to indicate he was part of the organization. A typical New Mexico greeting of "Hello friend, what can I help you with?"

Chile Charlie responded that he would like a guided tour of the facility.

Chile Charlie told Donald he had read and heard so much about Spaceport America that he thought he needed to take a guided tour.

Straight responded, "We would be glad to make arrangements, but it was unusual to do this without an invitation or prearrangement tour."

However, Mr. Straight started his orientation tour by giving Chile Charlie the spaceport's mission. "The Spaceport provides a supportive home for commercial space tenants and customers. So, they can contribute to the industry and inspire and delight our visitors."

Next, Donald Straight explained, "Spaceport America was the world's first purposely built commercial spaceport. The FAA-licensed launch complex was situated on 18,000 acres adjacent to the US Army White Sands Missile Range. It boasts 6000 square miles of restricted airspace, low population density, a 12,000-foot runway, and 340+ days of sunshine and low humidity. Some of the most respected companies in the commercial space industry are housed here.

Mr. Straight said with his chest expanding with pride, "Some of our customers include Virgin Galactic, SpaceX, UP Aerospace, and now the EXOS. EXOC is a company that has decades of practical experience in suborbital reusable space launch vehicles."

He continued, "We are accepting the manifest launch requests for the 2022 calendar year. Virgin Galatic targets payload customers who want to "fly now" rather than a year from now. This move will require minutes of micro G time with Prompt access to their payload. The first flight with Richard Branson on board was taken July 2021."

Donald explained, "This brief orientation is all I can give you today." He continued, "You should've stopped at the Hatch Information Center to get a schedule of guided tours of the facility. The facility has a strict policy against individual tours."

Chile Charlie was disappointed, but policies are policies, and he found his El Camino ready to rumble back to Las Cruces. He vowed that he would return for one of the group-directed tours later.

On his way back to Las Cruces, he saw a sign that read, "Hatch, The Chile Capital of the World and the Home of the Best Green Chile Hamburgers." He remembered there was a Spaceport America information center in Hatch. He thought he could kill two birds in one stop.

He slowed down and exited into the small rustic village of Hatch. Chile Charlie had to decide whether to have a green Chile hamburger first or go to the Spaceport of America Information Center. He took a coin out of his pocket and flipped it high into the air. He would eat first and then go to the information center first. He held his breath, and the coin came up heads. The decision was made. Eat first. He founded the famous Hatch Café. He ordered a favorite green Chile hamburger with French fries and a large Coke. He was starving, so he devoured it in record time. He paid his bill and headed for the information center.

Once he entered the information center, his curiosity overwhelmed the volunteer agent. Chile Charlie could not stop looking at all the information about the American spaceport. After an hour of looking through all the files and pictures and talking to the volunteer tourist aid, he quickly returned to Las Cruces.

Once he arrived in Las Cruces, he could only think about his wonderful day. He would think about going back soon.

CHAPTER EIGHT

CHILE CHARLIE GOES TO LORDSBURG

Lordsburg: A spot in the road or a spot in US history.

It has been a coon's age since Chile Charlie had ventured out of the safe confines of Las Cruces. He had been watching Netflix movies for the past several weeks. One film featured the village of Lordsburg. He got out his Atlas and determined that the Village of Lordsburg was 120 miles west of Las Cruces.

He went to the nearest service station and filled up his gas tank. He drove back to his tent and loaded the back end of his El Camino with the necessary supplies for such a long trip. He took his styrofoam cooler, tent, tools, and dry food. He covered the back end of his El Camino with a tarp. He was ready to go. "Interstate ten and Lordsburg, here we come," he said.

But first, Chile Charlie had to get out his Boy Scout checklist. The last item was to check the oil in the El Camino before he took the gem of a vehicle out on the road. In doing so, the El Camino needed a quart of oil to bring it up to full. He put a quart of oil in the engine and was ready to get on the road.

At noon, Chile Charlie arrived at the turn-off for Deming. The hunger pangs knocked on his brain. He turned off and proceeded to downtown Deming. He found a lovely-looking eating establishment. The sign read Paula's Fine Mexican Meals. Chile Charlie walked into Paula's restaurant and was quickly seated at a checkerboard red and white tablecloth. The waitress, who was tall and thin, came up and asked him, "What would you like to drink?"

He said, "Water with lemon but no ice."

The waitress left a menu and returned with a massive glass of water, a lemon, and no ice.

"Have you decided what you would like for lunch today," the waitress asked.

Chile Charlie said yes, "I want your world-famous Eggplant Parmesan with Marinara sauce."

After a wait that seemed like an eternity, Chile Charlie got his order. He ate ferociously because he was famished. He demolished the food, drank water, ate the lemon, and requested his check. After paying, he jumped into his El Camino and started the next step in the Lordsburg trip.

Chile Charlie was surprised when he read a sign that he was crossing over the Continental Divide. He got out of the vehicle and looked around.

What he saw was space with a faint rise in the land. That was all. There was not any divide he could see except the sign.

It took an hour and a half to get from Deming to Lordsburg.

When Chile Charlie finally arrived in Lordsburg proper, he looked for the local Chamber of Commerce office. The office was in a small shack-like building just off Main Street. He walked in and introduced himself to Maria Smallbox, the director.

She was petite with a round face, silken black hair, and a tan from the sun that shined 24/7 on the village of Lordsburg. She wore an off-the-shoulder blouse and a colorful flowing skirt in Southwest style.

After some preliminary information exchange, Chile Charlie asked Maria to give him some basic history of Lordsburg. She stated, "Lordsburg dates to 1880 when the Southern Pacific Railroad came through the village from the West. The original camp grew with an influx of railroad workers, freighters, miners, cowboys, ranchers, gamblers, and merchants.

"The village could have taken its name from Dr. Charles H. Lord, a New York native. He came west during the Civil War to become one of Tucson's leading businessmen. He and a partner started banking and wholesale businesses and shipped products along the railroad. It could've also been taken from Delbert Lord, Southern Pacific Railroad's chief engineer during its construction."

Director Smallbox got up from behind her desk and slowly walked to a stack of brochures. She picked up one entitled Gateway to the Southwest. She handed it to Chile Charlie, saying, "Here is a brochure that will give you information about current events happening in our village." Then, she slowly returned to her desk to continue her historical description of Lordsburg.

Marie continued with the history: "Lordsburg was important in freight hauling. Not only did the Southern Pacific Railroad, but the Butterfield Stage route passed through Mexican Springs, what is now Shakespeare. Then, in 1858, John Butterfield created an overland mail and passenger company with 250 coaches, one thousand horses, five hundred mules, and about eight hundred employees. The Butterfield Stage route avoided the more inclement weather further north. It ran through Stern, Benson, Arizona,

Tucson, Arizona, Yuma, Arizona, and to San Francisco and Los Angeles."

Maria leaned back in her chair and said, "Lordsburg made its name as the stop at the junctions of Highways 70 and 80, major roads in New Mexico. Lordsburg was featured on Broadway of the American Highway, a TV Series, and in 1964, Lordsburg boasted twenty-one motels, twenty cafeterias, and thirty-one service stations. Lordsburg was the biggest gas, food, and lodging stop between Arizona and Texas."

Miss Smallbox looked like she was in a dream when she said, "Lordsburg was the destination in the movie *Stagecoach*, the ninth greatest Western film of all time. According to the American Film Institute, this revelation was starring John Wayne. It was Wayne's breakthrough role as Ringo Kid, directed by John Ford. "Then, in 1995, this film was deemed culturally, historically, and statically significant by the United States Library of Congress and selected for preservation in the National Film Registry.

"The town of Lordsburg is mentioned twenty times in the movie. Then, in 1965, Lordsburg was cited as the main town, and the cinema Apache Uprising starred Rory Calhoun, Corrine Calvert, Lon Chaney Junior, and Jean Evans.

"In the book *When the "Emperor Was Divine*, a father is mentioned as having been taken away to Lordsburg internment camp during World War II. In the book *Interred with Their Bones* by Jennifer Lee Carrel, Lordsburg is mentioned as near the ghost town of Shakespeare, part of the protagonist's search. In the story, the character flew into the airport in Lordsburg.

"You can see, Chile Charlie; Lordsburg has been in films and books for a long time. We may be small, but we were recognized," Marie said.

Charlie started to read the brochure that the director gave him. In the latest census, he discovered that the village of Lordsburg had three thousand souls. There has been a slight increase in people because the US Border Patrol has increased its presence in the Bootheel section of New Mexico.

He found out in his reading that Lordsburg was the birthplace of the official New Mexico state song, "O Fair New Mexico." Lordsburg resident Elizabeth Garrett, the blind daughter of the fame Sheriff Pat Garrett, wrote it. 1917 Governor Washington Ellsworth Lindsay signed the legislation, making it the official state song. In 1928, John Philip Sousa arranged the state song embraced in a musical story of the Indian, Cavalry, Spanish, and Mexican people.

Chile Charlie has always been interested in flying. In 1927, Lindburg landed in Lordsburg. Charlie also learned that in December 1938, the Lordsburg Municipal Airport became officially operational. It was the first recognized airport in New Mexico.

In the early 1950s, the original Frontiers Airline served the airport. Their DC3s landed in Lordsburg from El Paso to Phoenix.

The brochure had a section about Lordsburg's history during World War II. A prisoner-of-war camp held 1500 Japanese Americans. The United States Army operated the Japanese American internment camp.

On July 27, 1942, shortly after the Lordsburg internment camp was opened, Private Burleson, a sentry at the facility, allegedly shot two Japanese American internees under questionable circumstances. One victim, Hirota Isomura, died instantly. The other died before dawn. After a military investigation and court-martial, Burleson was found to have lawfully killed the two men. The incident inspired an episode of the new Hawaii 50 series. Captive German and Italian soldiers were held there. The camp operated until July 1943.

Maria said, "Lordsburg has been a popular rest stop for people traveling to and from the West Coast by car on Interstate 10 for many years. Lordsburg's hotels had one of the few areas wherein the Southwest would accept blacks. It was especially popular with African American travelers in the mid-20th century during the end of legal segregation. El Paso, Texas, was the other community in the Southwest to accept black travelers in hotels."

Marie changed gears when she asked Charlie if he had ever heard of the ghost town, Shakespeare.

Chile Charlie answered, "No!"

Maria saw the opening and pronounced, "Ghost towns abound in New Mexico. Most are memories of what they once were, not much more than Remington's of an old building or rounded mounds of melted Adobe walls. A few have survived the ravages of time and have been rescued by preservationists. Shakespeare is one such town.

"Located a couple of miles southwest of Lordsburg, Shakespeare was founded in 1870 when prospectors discovered silver in lobes close enough to the surface for easy mining. Within a short while, the town had a hundred and seventy buildings and a population of over three thousand.

"Once the easy ore gave out, people began leaving. The town was in decline. The cross-country railroad and a spur belt from the mainline in Lordsburg had been completed by then. The railroad made it economical to mine lower-grade silver ore, shipping it to a smelter elsewhere. Shakespeare's population is stabilized at two hundred fifty people.

"You can see the restored buildings as you pass by on Interstate 10," said Marie. There is an entrance fee collected in a small box. It's like a donation to keep the facility in pristine condition."

Chile Charlie relaxed when a thump came on the front door and walked a character dressed in border patrol green. He was tall, good-looking, and straight as an arrow, walking with dignity into the Chamber of Commerce office. He said in a Mississippi drawl, "Good afternoon, Miss Smallbox." "And how is the village doing today?"

"The village is in good hands and doing very well today, Commander Durling."

"I would like you to meet Chile Charlie from the great city of Las Cruces."

"Chile Charlie, this is Commander Ray Durling of the United States Border Control."

"Good to meet you, Commander Durling," Chile Charlie replied.

Commander Durling looked Chile Charlie up and down. Then he thought he might invite this character to visit Antelope Wells, which would get Chile Charlie deeper into the Bootheel of New

Mexico. Antelope Wells was about forty-five miles directly south of Lordsburg and was the lonely crossing point between the United States and Mexico. The community consisted of a handful of American citizens and two hundred fifty border patrol agents responsible for guarding the entryway into the United States.

After mentally evaluating Chile Charlie, the commander asked, "Chile Charlie, would you like to visit Antelope Wells?"

Considering the invitation by such a high-ranking border patrol agent, Chile Charlie accepted the invitation with one consideration. That consideration was that the Border Patrol would provide him with potable water.

Chile Charlie thanked Miss Marie for all her valuable information about the village of Lordsburg. He strolled out to his El Camino, opened his map, and started his journey to Antelope Wells.

It was now six p.m. Chile Charlie was getting hungry. He pulled over and made camp for the evening. Charlie pitched his tent for the evening.

Next, he removed the food chest, started a small campfire, opened a can of pork and beans, and made himself a ham salad sandwich.

Chile Charlie felt good about being in the open, free of people, places, and things. He just wanted to contemplate what he had learned about the village of Lordsburg.

He only wanted to have time to himself. Looking around, he saw a small village just south of his campsite. He glanced at his map. It was Hachita. He decided to spend the morning looking around this abandoned community. Meanwhile, Charlie looked at the sky, wondering how many stars were in space. He was amazed at the cloudless sky.

The sun was on the horizon as Chile Charlie gathered his wits about him and left his comfortable sleeping tent. He prepared his breakfast of beans and cornbread. To him, it was an exciting first-class cowboy breakfast. After breakfast, he explored the ghost town only a few hundred steps from his camp.

What he found was just marvelous. A refurbished church was serving the area's Catholic population and community center. There was nothing else in the abandoned town. He looked inside the church to see if the front door was unlocked. It was open, and in he went. It was beautiful, with the sunlight coming through the colored windows and the pulpit that looked like it had been there for hundreds of years.

Upon leaving the church, Charlie continued his trip southwest to the small community of Rodeo. It was about twenty miles southwest of his present location. He estimated it would take him thirty-five minutes to arrive.

Once he got to Rodeo with its fifteen households, he found an unusual community art gallery that also served as the local post office. The rodeo had a community tagline of "Gateway to the Chiricahua Mountains."

While Chile Charlie talked to the Community Gallery Director Angle Costa and learned about Rodeo's history.

"Rodeo was founded in 1902 as a rail stop for the El Paso and Southwestern Railroad line. It ran from Bisbee, Arizona, to El Paso, Texas. The town became the center for cattle shipping in the San Simon Valley. Two views exist as to the source of Rodeo's name. One suggests it derives from the Spanish word *rodeo*, meaning roundup or enclosure, about cattle shipping. However, the noun *rodeo* derives from the Spanish verb order, meaning surround or go around. The El Paso and Southwestern Railroad runs east across the southern part of the state. After passing through Antelope

Pass, it turns south to Rodeo, continues to Douglas, Arizona, and then north to Bisbee, going around the Chiricahua Mountains," Angle said.

After lunch with Angele, Chile Charlie was headed for Antelope Wells, twenty-five miles away. He packed his gear, got into his El Camino, and left.

The road was narrow, graveled, and dusty. It was slow going because of all the potholes and dust. The journey took over an hour.

Charlie immediately went to the Border Patrol Checkpoint. He saw a small rectangular structure without a painting in the last twenty years. This checkpoint had no distinguishing characteristics that would make it look like a substantial United States official welcoming structure.

Chile Charlie asked for the commanding agent of the facility. Agent Sam Hernandez stepped forward to shake Charlie's extended hand.

Agent Hernandez was a short, fat, hyper man of about forty-five years old. He welcomed Charlie to the Antelope Wells Border Patrol Checkpoint.

In Charlie's most dignified and curious voice, he asked Agent Hernandez if he could give them a quick synopsis of the Antelope Wells checkpoint.

Agent Sam Hernandez answered, "Antelope Wells is in Hidalgo County, New Mexico. The community is located along the Mexico – United States border in the New Mexico Bootheel region. Despite its name, there are neither antelope nor wells in the area. The name comes from an old ranch two and a half miles north. The only inhabitants are four immigrant families and United States Customs and Border Protection employees."

After Agent Hernandez checked the lonely road south, he continued, "Antelope Wells is the southernmost settlement of New Mexico. The village is in the region commonly known as the Bootheel of New Mexico. It is the smallest and least-used border crossing of the forty-three ports of entry along the border with Mexico. The crossing is open solely for non-commercial traffic every day from 10:00 AM to 4:00 PM."

Then Agent Hernandez said, "The port was established by Ulysses S. Grant in 1872 and has been staffed since 1928. In 1981, the community had a population of two families living in a trailer behind the customs station.

An average of three people per day enter the United States at the checkpoint. In 2019, only ninety-three pedestrians crossed the border. Including domestic and international travelers, fewer than two hundred buses and privately owned vehicles pass through the checkpoint each month. Traffic increased in 2020 with more international shuttle van services. Despite its low usage, there is no move to close the port. Antelope Wells provides the most direct route from the United States to the Sierra Madre Occidental."

"Boy," Chile Charlie said, "What a fascinating brief history of such an out-of-the-way checkpoint."

Agent Franzoy came into the checkpoint office breathless. He said, "It's official. The rogue quarter horse race is on for tonight."

"What," Chile Charlie asked, "is a rogue quarter horse race?"

Agent Franzoy stated, "The area's environment was dotted with a human population of 0+1 density, which meant there weren't many people surrounding Antelope Wells. There were no cinemas, shopping malls, or Disneyland. There was only open space. So those who lived here had to create their entertainment and diversion from the monotonous life of this area."

He said, "Those who lived here were also high-stakes gamblers." Some ingenious Mexican and

American ranchers had the idea of Mexican quarter horses racing against American quarter horses along a short stretch of the Mexican-American border. The barbed wire fence could be a racing lane for the horses. A brilliant idea of entertainment for the surrounding population was hatched.

Agent Hernandez asked, "Charlie if he wants to stay the evening and watch the upcoming quarter horse races."

It didn't take Chile Charlie but a few New York seconds to stay and watch those races.

Hernandez told Charlie they would start at nine o'clock. That meant they wouldn't start until after dark.

Chile Charlie asked, "How are they going to see?"

Agent Hernandez laughingly told Charlie, "You wait and see the innovative, creative forces these ranchers have created."

It was nearly seven o'clock, and Charlie had two hours to spare before the first three-quarter horse races. The question of what to do lingered in the back of Charlie's mind. He found himself in a place without apparent tourist attractions, with no specific time or location to explore.

Charlie decided the best thing was to wait and watch the lizards play hide and seek with each other.

A dust storm emerged from the south and the north at nine o'clock. The source of these dust storms was eight Ford 150 pickup trucks, four approaching from the north and four from the south. Each pickup towed a horse trailer. They strategically positioned themselves to encompass the quarter-mile racetrack in both directions. The owners of the pickups turned on their headlights, casting light upon the racetrack.

The wagering for the first race was now underway. There was much squabbling and quarreling and heated exchange of words between the Americans and the Mexicans. One horse from each side was unloaded and taken to the starting line.

Each horse was impatiently prancing up and down until a shot rang out, and the race began. Each horse was running at full speed. The Mexican horse was declared the winner. Devastation took place on the American side with all the money lost during the first race.

Chile Charlie continued to watch the next two races. It was now midnight. Chile Charlie decided to retire to his tent, get up early in the morning, and head back to the paradise surroundings of Las Cruces. So off he goes into his El Camino, heading east on Railroad Road to Columbus, north to Deming, and East to Las Cruces. His long trip to Lordsburg ended. Chile Charlie was exhilarated and exhausted from everything he had experienced the last few days.

CHAPTER NINE

CHILE CHARLIE DISCOVERS PLAYAS

Chile Charlie was getting very restless in his quest for knowledge. He wanted to learn about another small village in the Bootheel region. To fill the bill, Charlie got out his trusty Rand McNally Atlas. He examined it for a long time. Finally, Playas would be his destination.

Chile Charlie got out his checklist for the necessities of a three or four-day trip to explore the village of Playas. He needed a tent, sleeping bag, clean clothes, a three-day supply of food, and extra gasoline for the El Camino.

Charlie took Interstate 10 West until he found the sixty-eight-mile marker. The El Camino purred like a finely oiled sewing machine down Interstate 10 at the blazing speed of sixty-five mph. Chile

Charlie was thrilled as he gazed at the stark, barren landscape.

Then, he turned south and took county roads to his destination, Playas.

Chile Charlie arrived in Playas at 11:30 in the morning. He looked around and was amazed at the town's cleanliness and orderliness. There were people everywhere in various modes of dress. Some look like ranchers, others look like law officers in uniforms, and others look like ordinary male and female community members. The astounding part of the population was the lack of children and teenagers. Charlie drove up and down the streets until he found the post office.

He got out of his El Camino and went inside. He asked if he could see the postmaster. He was ushered into the post office's back area, where he met a person dressed in a United Postal Service uniform.

The person said, "My name is Billy Armejo. I am the postmaster for the village of Playas; how can I help you?"

Chile Charlie said, "I am on an adventure to learn about the history, culture, and what makes a place like Playas tick.

Billy asked Charlie, "Why do you want to know this information?"

Charlie said, "I am writing an informational book about unusual ghost towns and small communities in the Bootheel Region of New Mexico."

Billy told Charlie to sit down and make himself comfortable. Then Billy asked Charlie, "Would you like a cup of boiled coffee that tastes like it was made several days ago?"

Charlie answered in the affirmative.

Billy stated, "Playas was a former company town named after a nearby settlement along the Southern Pacific Railroad. The Phelps Dodge Corporation developed the company town in the 1970s for its then-new Hidalgo Copper Smelter employees, located ten miles south of Playas."

Charlie was impressed and said, "Go on."

Billy continued, "The community had over 270 rental homes, six apartment buildings, a post office, a grocery/dry goods store, a medical clinic with a heliport, a bowling alley ("Copper Pins"), a grill, a rodeo arena, horse stables, a fitness center, a shooting range, an airstrip, and a swimming pool.

"Playas even had its own ZIP Code (88009). The town had about 1,100 residents at its peak and included two churches built on land leased from the mining company."

Charlie sipped his hot coffee and asked Billy, "Why was the village abandoned?"

Billy renewed his explanation, "The company closed the smelter as part of moving towards new processing technologies for processing copper concentrates.

"The declining copper prices accelerated the closure. Its residents were required to leave within a year. A skeleton crew of about a dozen employees remained in the area.

"Before razing the plant and reclamation of the site, the smelter was nicknamed *La Estrella del Norte* by unauthorized migrants. They used its lights as a beacon for crossing into the United States."

Charlie was shocked by this bit of information. He then asked Billy, "What happened to Playas?"

Billy declared, " New Mexico Tech agreed to purchase the town four years later. The town is now a training and research facility (the Playas Training and Research Center, operated by New Mexico Tech's EMRTC) for the University's first responders and counter-terrorism programs, supported by tens of millions of dollars in federal funds."

Chile Charlie queried, "You mean to tell me that a university bought the total town?"

"Yes, that is what I meant."

Billy looked at his watch and said, I must close the post office to take my kids to Little League baseball practice. I will not be available until about eleven o'clock tomorrow."

There was no hotel or public camping area in Playas. Charlie found the local law enforcement office and asked to pitch his tent in the public park area since he had to stay overnight. The officer said that would be fine and would check on Charlie during the evening hours. Next, Charlie made himself a spam sandwich and his dinner by the light of the moon.

The following day, he got up, washed his face and hands, and changed his shirt. He strolled around the community, looking at the structures. Charlie conceded that the community buildings were being put to practical use.

At eleven o'clock sharp, Charlie entered the post office to find Mr. Armijo at his desk writing his description of the new use for the village of Playas.

Billy started his storytelling by giving Charlie his interpretation of what it was like to take some Playas Training and Research Center training.

With all the melodrama that a good storyteller would use, he started his conversation, "The smell of roasting goat and the dry earth floor beneath exquisite carpets is a constant reminder that you are not in Kansas anymore.

The morning air echoes with the local Pashto, while a gentle breeze carries the traditional attire, 'qmis' and 'shahwar,' worn by the men heading to the 'shura.'

He continued, "It brings back the feeling of being in Afghanistan," said one officer who had served two tours. The sensory input overwhelmed the present and transported him to another time and place. For a soldier readying to go to Afghanistan for the first time, "It gives me a feeling of what it will be like. I'm trained, but this helped me understand the people's aspect more.

"Soldiers in this realistic training find that their adrenaline rushes when there are rumors of Taliban members infiltrating the village or shots fired during the night. "It's not real, but your body thinks it is. You get into the moment, and it's no longer playing.

"Interacting with native Afghans is also a revelation. They are peace-loving people with much honor in their traditions. Learning how to treat them is very valuable." Sitting in a "shura" and knowing when to speak and how to show respect are some of the skills learned in realistic training."

Charlie said that was interesting. "Is there any other information that I should know?"

Billy handed Charlie a pamphlet; Charlie took down the significant points. They were:

Develop complex training scenarios that accurately replicate specific areas of operation within the theaters of war in Iraq, Afghanistan, and the Horn of Africa.

Create an authentic hyper-immersive training environment to allow the training audience maximum opportunities to achieve its objectives.

- Train US Special Operations and conventional US Military Forces; over five thousand were trained in 2010.

- Integration of joint tactical enablers supporting the distributed operation.
- Joint distributed lethal and non-lethal combat operations.
- Airborne insertions (free fall static line and heavy drop).
- Air Assault insertions.
- Close air support (JTAC) training.
- Long-distance communications.
- Sniper live fire and high-angle live firing
- Desert driving and land navigation techniques.
- Long-distance cross-country land navigation training.
- Live demolition training up to 10000 lbs. explosives.
- Rock climbing and desert survival techniques.
- Occupy COP in an eastern urban setting.
- Role player and Key leader engagements replicating shuras /jurgas found in Southwest and Central Asia and the Horn of Africa.
- High-altitude desert survival.

- Counter IED and Attack the Network training, replicating IED networks found in Iraq, Afghanistan, and Iran.
- Joint special operations mission training; mission-specific pre-deployment training.
- Village Stability Operations (VSO).
- Interagency integration within a tactical staff; non-lethal aspects of planning and executing combat operations.
- Computer network attack and network exploitation.
- Signals intelligence collection (GSM, PTT, and HPCP).
- Human intelligence collection (Military Source Operations, Recruited Sources, Tactical interrogations).
- Law Enforcement Professional integration into staff operations.
- Instrumented AAR support with capture video and audio support available.

- On-site, 10-60 seat, fully instrumented classrooms.
- SCIF supportable; classified work area available.

What People Say...

-->"There was a flexible storyboard, unscripted events, and real third and fourth-order effects."

-->"Training in a COIN environment provided us with a realistic situation in Afghanistan."

-->"Immersion in the realistic environment provided significantly more learning than a much greater time frame of traditional instruction."

Chile Charlie picked up his notepad and placed it in his knapsack. He turned to Mr. Armijo and said, "You gave ample information about the Village of Playas. Thank you very much for your hospitality. I must return to Camp Hope in Las Cruces now."

"I would like to stay in touch if that would be OK with you."

Billy declared, "It would be my pleasure to stay in touch with you, Chile Charlie."

With that pronouncement, Charlie walked to his El Camino and left Playas.

CHAPTER TEN

CHILE CHARLIE GOES RACING

It started 38 years ago! "What do you mean it started 38 years ago?" asked Chile Charlie of Joe Merchant, who looked like Ichabod Crain with his long neck and deep-set dark eyes.

"When I said it, I meant that was Deming, New Mexico's trademark event, THE GREAT AMERICAN DUCK RACE," exclaimed Joe.

"The news about the 38th Annual Great American Duck Race is spreading like the wildfires in the mountains of California. There is news about this event everywhere you turn. The not-for-profit Great American Duck Race Incorporated marketing committee has done an excellent job getting the word out.

Over the years, people worldwide, like Russia, China, Pakistan, Europe, and the Middle East, have ventured into the City of Deming to partake in this unusual event."

Chile Charlie hitched up his trousers, turned away from Joe, and said, "Adios;" "I'm heading for Deming, New Mexico, to check out the Great American Duck Races."

Chile Charlie got into his El Camino to travel sixty miles west of Las Cruces to the sleepy small town of Deming. He hadn't been outside the city limits for over twenty minutes when he encountered his first obstacle. The Border Patrol checkpoint loomed ahead. He was afraid they would want to check for contraband because he was in the El Camino--drugs. But he was mistaken. The friendly Border Patrol agent waved him on, and away Chile Charlie went to Deming.

When he arrived in Deming, the first thing that Chile Charlie did was to find someone who could give him the background about the duck races. He went to the local restaurant and found Marie Lockport alone at the counter. She was a longtime Deming resident. She was a petite young lady in her early fifties. She did not look like she belonged in this rural community. But as Chile Charlie talked to Marie, he discovered that she had lived in Deming all her life and was a treasure trove of information about the Great American duck race.

First, Marie gave Chile Charlie a brief history of how the races originated.

She mentioned, "Deming is a small, sleepy town that thirty-eight years ago sought to inject some excitement to Deming's identity. The origins of this event are a bit murky--some claim it started with four individuals at a bar, while others say it began with four people in a restaurant. Another account suggests that four guys in the backroom of the Deming Newspaper (The Headlight) hatched the idea for the most unusual event. One fact not in dispute is that the editor of the Deming Newspaper was the driving force behind getting the first race off and waddling.

Next, Marie gave rambling information about the upcoming event, which will start soon. She said: "It's that time of year when thousands of people migrate and flock to Deming to the Annual Great American Duck Race. The theme of this year's races, which marks thirty-eight years of duck celebrations in Deming, will be "Beach Party Duck." Visitors can expect the same wacky, family-friendly fun at this year's Great American Duck Race. Still, organizers hope adding several new attractions will make the events more enjoyable."

With her hand on her hip, looking like a middle linebacker of the Denver Broncos, Marie said, "The events will take place from Thursday, Aug. 25 to Sunday, Aug. 28, at various locations in the community. The main attractions center is at the Luna County Courthouse, 700 South Silver Avenue. They call it McKinley Duck Downs."

Chile Charlie was intrigued about the conduct of the duck race and asked Marie if she had any pictures, and she said she just had one taken last year. And Chile Charlie looked at it in amazement.

Courtesy of Great American Duck Race, Inc

By this time, Chile Charlie was getting too much information and asked Marie if she would tell him what it costs and what happens to the money raised for this event.

Maria explained, "A portion of the proceeds from sales will go back to the Duck Race Committee to help organize future events. Entry to the races is always free; however, it costs $5 to enter a racing duck. Races this year will include wet and dry races and a separate prize for each category of race."

"It's a huge community event, and it's been running for so long that it has become a staple of Deming. It's a trademark of Deming, the 'Deming Duck Races.' With that pronouncement, Chile Charlie promised Marie Lockport that he would return with his $5.00 to race his rented duck.

CHAPTER ELEVEN

CHILE CHARLIE RACES DUCKS

The third Saturday in August arrived. It was time for Chile Charlie to get into his El Camino to travel west again to Deming. People came from the East, West, North, and South to participate in the Great American Duck Race. Chile Charlie didn't care about anything; he just wanted to participate in a duck race. He took a beat-up $20 bill he thought he could invest in the races. He knew that he would win. But so did everybody else who attended. Everybody thought they would win.

When he initially reached the duck race venue at the old Courthouse Square, he spent the first hour exploring the various vendors. They offered food, clothes, gadgets, and Great American Duck Race souvenirs. Being frugal, he was reluctant to spend any portion of his $20 bill. Despite the tempting array of goods, nothing caught his interest except for the featured food of fried turkey leg that was big enough for lunch and some leftovers. The turkey legs were huge.

It was nearing time to get registered for the duck races. As Chile Charlie stepped up to pay his registration fee, he discovered Ms. Mary Lou Oblinger had been registering participants for the last 20 years. Mary Lou was a little overweight. Her beautiful facial contours made her popular with the race crowd. Her eyes were a heavenly blue color that stood out like a night beacon. Her hair was a golden brown with a complexion to match.

Chile Charlie got in line to register to pay his ten dollars for two ducks. He had difficulty deciding whether to race his rented duck on land or water. Finally, after flipping a coin, it was water. Over the loudspeaker came the number forty-four. That was Chile Charlie's number.

He rushed to the Duck Wrangler and was handed this wonderful-looking, speedy duck with a two-tone brown color. He cuddled the duck in his arms and talked to him in Midwestern lingo. He was unsure the duck understood one word he was speaking about because he thought the duck only knew Spanish. Chile Charlie knew only a few Hispanic phrases like Uno for one or Tres for three.

Now, it came time for his race to begin. This starter bellowed, "Are you ready on the right-- Are you ready on the left? Get set-- and go!" Chile Charlie dropped his duck in the water and watched its speed towards the finish line. Unfortunately, someone dropped a few kernels of corn in the water in Charlie's Duck's Lane. Chile Charlie's duck decided it was more important to eat those kernels of corn than to continue the race. Chile Charlie's duck came in and was called dead last. Chile Charlie was devastated because he wanted to win that race in the worst way.

He still had a ticket to rent a second duck. The procedure was the same. He had to wait until his number 227 was called to claim his rented duck. Chile Charlie marched up like a man on a mission to the Duck Wrangler to accept his rented duck. He was handed this beautiful, sleek, two-tone brown duck with a streak of black feathers from his bill to his chest. Charlie strolled to the starting line much like a confident person would. He waited for the starter to give the command to release your ducks.

Again, Chile Charlie was confident his duck would be the first to cross the finish line. The starter yelled to the duck racers, are you ready? Then he said so everyone could hear, "Start your ducks. Off the ducks went. Chile Charlie's duck did not finish in the running to progress to the next level on Sunday. That was okay with Chile Charlie because

he wanted to get back to Las Cruces for his supper--
the remaining portion of his vast turkey leg.

Off he went to find his El Camino truck and
return to Las Cruces with a once-in-a-lifetime
experience under his belt of racing ducks. All he
could think of was how much fun he had. It was a
fantastic day for Chile Charlie. In a few weeks, he
would be active with new experiences in Old West
Country.

CHAPTER TWELVE

CHILE CHARLIE BECOMES A HERO

Chile Charlie has been out of circulation for some
time, and there needs to be an explanation for his
sudden disappearance. If you will remember, his
last adventure was a trip to The Great American

Duck Race in Deming. Chile Charlie's duck did not finish in the running to progress to the next level on Sunday.

However, misfortune found its place with Chile Charlie on his return to Las Cruces. As he was traveling east on Interstate 10, there was a horrific pileup of cars in front of him. He stopped to assist. He rushed around several cars that were not damaged to find a young lady with four children in a severely damaged vehicle. Two other volunteers and Chile Charlie forced the passenger side door open and extricated the young lady from her seatbelt. They got her out of the car before any further damage to her could be done.

Next, the two men got the four young children out of their car seats and safely placed them on the ground. Chile Charlie and his two volunteer helpers proceeded further to the front of the crash site. They found a pickup truck that had rolled over onto its side. Gasoline was pouring out of the truck, causing great concern for the three men. Through brute force, the men got the pickup truck upright and opened the door. Unfortunately, the available side was the passenger side. A jolly 200-pound plus and the deadweight driver was strapped in his seat belt on the driver's side. It wasn't easy to reach down to unloose the seatbelts. Chile Charlie gingerly entered the cab and tried desperately to unfasten this safety belt. Unable to do so, he called for his friends to see if there was a knife he could cut the safety belt to extract the driver.

Fortunately, one of his friends did have a sharp pocket knife, and he cut the strap to release the driver from his predicament. The problem arose to get the driver out of the cab before the gasoline ignited. The driver was a jolly 200-pound person and deadweight. What was Chile Charlie to do? He couldn't lift the injured driver and was concerned about the leaking gasoline. He called for one of the other volunteers to enter the cab to see if the two could lift the injured driver out of the window.

With much effort by both men, the driver was finally extricated from the cab. Chile Charlie was pleased with his life-saving activities.

Charlie decided to return to his El Camino and continue his trip to Las Cruces. As he got ready to step into his El Camino, tragedy struck. A drunken driver was unaware of the flashing lights from the police cars and ambulances and crashed headlong into Chile Charlie's El Camino truck. Charlie was severely injured. Fortunately, the paramedics got him airlifted to an El Paso hospital. He remained at the hospital for over two months before he was released. He convalesced at a nursing home in Las Cruces for three months, taking physical therapy and checking for internal injuries.

When Chile Charlie was released from the nursing home, he did not want to do any traveling.

But his desire to explore the great state of New Mexico came back to life. He wanted to take trips to Mountainaire and Silver City to explore the life and adventures of Billy the Kid.

CHAPTER THIRTEEN

ON THE ROAD AGAIN

Chile Charlie decided that his next travel adventure would be to go to Mountainair, New Mexico. Mountainair is in the center of the Abo National Forest. He traveled across backcountry roads that would have had traffic jams if the two cars had met simultaneously. There was nothing out there but flat roads and a bird sometimes. It was very peaceful.

Chile Charlie discovered the history of Mountainair on the Internet. He decided to add this information to his story about the town. *The history of Mountainair and the surrounding area merges with its present-day description, offering a Gateway to Ancient Cities.*

Hundreds of years ago, Abó had an abundant water supply, creating a sustainable farming community that historians estimate may have reached 20,000 native inhabitants. A Pueblo (Tompiro) petroglyph at Abó, dated from the 1400s, depicts Tawa, the Sun-Father, one of the most revered deities of the Pueblo Indians, an essential element for a bountiful harvest. Abó is positioned on a major east-west trade route, the Abó Pass, a shallow gap that divides the Manzano and Los Piños Mountains.

The community of Abó was still thriving when Spanish explorers came upon it in 1561. Abó was the head of one of the most significant missionary operations in New Mexico, known today as part of the National Monument Salinas Pueblo Missions. The three sites comprising these ruins — Abó, Quarai, and Gran Quivira — attract historians, archeologists, and visitors to Mountainair worldwide.

Among the intriguing aspects of Mountainair are residents who can still tell the story of when their

Grandparents called an area within Monte Alto. However difficult it was to locate historic documents verifying these tales, one can only imagine a small village of settlers, unaware of the attention they were about to receive.

The attention arrived with the railroad and the founding of Mountainair by John Corbett, Colonel E.C. Manning, and former U.S. Governor E. S. Stover in 1903. It was the first incorporated town in the area–before Torrance was a county and New Mexico officially became a state. Strategically sited for the railroad at the summit of Abó Pass and named for its cool, fresh mountain breezes, passengers first rolled into Mountainair in 1907. They continued to travel during the 1960s. This alternate route, now primarily used for freight, known as the Belen cut-off, is part of the transcontinental tracks. It was built to alleviate the extreme grades and delays over the Raton and Glorietta passes. The depot owned by BNSF is listed on the National Register of Historic Places.

In the early 1900s, with rain in abundance, farming again played an essential role in the area's history, fostering a boom in the economy and increasing the population to 5,000. This entitled Mountainair became the "The Pinto Bean Capital of the World," housing the nation's largest bean processing center, with peak production reaching over 750 train carloads of beans in one season. Pinto beans, a sturdy crop, gave American soldiers their main rations through WWII. The beans were farmed on approximately 40,000 acres, using the rain as their principal water source. 1946, a ten-year drought began, leaving the land barren and forcing farmers to become ranchers or move to better living. With ranching being the mainstay in Torrance County, the population is 2,000+ in Mountainair, with more cattle than people living around the town.

In the mid-1980s, a resurgence of relocation to Mountainair occurred and continues today, with numerous new or renovated homes and businesses in

Mountainair and several innovative sub-divisions surrounding the town.

Mountainair's long and diverse history and the breathtaking views of the Chupadera Mesa and the Manzano Mountains have a mystique that captures the imagination of writers, artists, photographers, and individuals.

An hour from Albuquerque, Mountainair, Gateway to Ancient Cities offers an adventure into times past, enjoyment to its visitors, and endearment to its residents.

This was a sightseeing trip for Chile Charlie to see the refurbished and historic Shafer Hotel. Chile Charlie visited the Shafter Hotel, which is on the national register of landmark hotels.

He learns that the hotel was built in 1823. Mr. Shafer, who moved to Mountain Air in 1908, renovated it. The hotel stands as a landmark and tourist attraction all on its own. Some have said that

Pop Shafter still roams the hallways today. The hotel has been recently remodeled without losing its quaint charm and historical importance. The rooms are arranged from a simple cowboy room with a community bathroom to an elegant wedding sweet with two bathtubs and a wet bar. All rooms are furnished with antique furniture. The outdoor park has an Art Deco gazebo and covered patio that adds much time to the number of weddings held there.

CHAPTER FOURTEEN

CHILE CHARLIE LEARNS ABOUT BILLY THE KID

During Chile Charlie's rehabilitation from his accident, he read many books about the times and experiences of Billy the Kid. Chile Charlie got the itch to explore towns that claim some of Billy the

Kid's folklore. Chile Charlie decided that he would make his first trip to Silver City. It is one hundred twenty miles north and west of Las Cruces, Chile Charlie's adopted home.

Upon arriving in Silver City late afternoon, he went to the Silver City Visitor's Center. The Service and Tourism Coordinator was Rebecca Martin. She was a delightful, talkative young lady who explained the virtues of Silver City as a lovely community.

Rebecca gave the following brief history of how Silver City got its name. "While the Spanish Santa Rita copper mines opened operations in 1805, the American silver strike of 1870 was the real inspiration for the town's name."

Then Rebecca explained, "The mining rush that built the town and brought miners and settlers into direct conflict with the local Apache tribes led by Victoria, Geronimo, and Cochise. Silver City got the reputation of the rough and tumble community."

Rebecca told Chile Charlie that Billy the Kid's family moved to Silver City when he was fourteen. She said, "There is a replication of his mother's home here." Chile Charlie asked Rebecca for directions to see Billy the Kid's mother's home.

After he got the directions to the house, he left and was stopped by a local character named Keith LeMay. Keith asked Chile Charlie if he were new to Silver City. The question took Chile Charlie back. Finally, he told Keith LeMay he was studying Billy the Kid's life. He was here to get more information. Keith, a personality and part-time historian, said he would help Chile Charlie if he wanted the help. Chile Charlie jumped at the chance to get more information from this person.

Keith began his oration with these words, "History knows Billy the Kid as a hothead with a hogleg. Chile Charlie was dumbfounded with the word hogleg. He said he knew what hothead meant but didn't know what hogleg meant. Mr. LeMay politely and condescendingly explained that a hogleg was a large single-action revolver that was the type carried by most Western cowboys.

Keith said, "Billy the Kid loved throwing us historians a curveball. For example, as a boy running the streets of Silver City, he was likable enough. But we now read of a photograph showing him playing the civilized game of croquet with Sadie."

Now Keith said with a twinkle in his eye, "That's not the end of the story of Billy the Kid and Silver City. In 1876, Billy the Kid visited San Elizario, a small town just east of Silver City, to break a friend out of jail. Interestingly, in 2010, there were reenactments of the event, guided tours of historic talks, and arts and crafts with highlights of Billy the Kid Festival on this exciting weekend piece. Grant County's Sheriff Harvey Whitehill wrote a brief description. Early newspaper accounts and a document in the Pinos Altos Museum show Billy the Kid's first practicing his jailbreaking skills at sixteen in Silver City.

Chile Charlie wanted to visit the museum but thought better of the side trip because it was getting late. He had to get back to Las Cruces before dark. Chile Charlie jumped into his El Camino to wing his way to the City of Crosses.

CHAPTER FIFTEEN

CHILE CHARLIE VISITS BILLY THE KID'S GRAVE

When we last talked to Chile Charlie, he was back in Las Cruces from Silver City. He got home in record time and spent several days in Las Cruces's Branigan Library studying the life and times of Billy the Kid.

He discovered that Billy the Kid was buried in Fort Sumner. He had accumulated enough money to buy gas for a quick trip to Billy the Kid's gravesite.

Chile Charlie thought he might even get to talk to the local people about the legend of Billy the Kid. Some say he had the fastest horse known to man or had a very energetic public relations and marketing genius worldwide.

Chile Charlie packed up his El Camino with three days' food provisions, his tent, his sleeping bag, and some tools for when his faithful El Camino would need tender loving care.

Charlie was in the process of figuring out the best route to reach his destination. He consulted an old United States Atlas and turned to the New Mexico section. After thoroughly examining all possible routes, it became clear that the most suitable path would lead him through Ruidoso and Roswell, taking him to Fort Sumner.

It took him four hours of steady driving to the outskirts of Fort Sumner. He looked up the Chamber of Commerce office first. As he walked in the door of the Chamber of Commerce, Chile Charlie was greeted by Director, Wayne Heppenstall. He was a throwback to an earlier generation. He wore a dark green athletic cut shirt with a blue bolo tie that is as casual as he gets during workdays and weekends. His white hair is neatly combed; his eyes, bright and alert, are framed by rimless glasses. He walks slower than he used to.

Chile Charlie said, "This is my first time visiting Fort Sumner, and I would like to learn its history."

Mr. Heppenstall said, "Sure," as he handed Chile Charlie a brochure about the town.

Then he said, "Fort Sumner is a village in De Baca County. The population is a thousand down two hundred people from the 2010 U.S. Census. Fort Sumner is the county seat of De Baca County and, in the spring and fall, is home of the Columbia Scientific Balloon Facility and the burial site of the famed outlaw of the American West, Billy the Kid, who was shot and killed here in 1881."

As an afterthought, Wayne said, "Fort Sumner was named after former New Mexico territory military governor Edwin Voss Sumner. Fort Sumner was a military fort charged with the internment of nearby Navajo and Mescalero Apache populations from 1863 to 1868. The federal government closed the Fort in 1868."

Chile Charlie thanked Mr. Heppenstall for all the information regarding the village of Fort Sumner.

"Now, how do I get to the cemetery where Billy the Kid was buried," Charlie asked.

Wayne said, "Go to the gas station, turn left, and follow the sidewalk two blocks, and you'll be there."

Chile Charlie walked.

On the way, he came across one of the local business people named Herman Strong Face. Mr. Strong Face asked if he needed any help. Chile Charlie said no, he would meander over to the cemetery where Billy the Kid was buried.

Herman told Chile Charlie he was an expert on Billy the Kid and would be happy to give Charlie insights into the life and times of Billy the Kid if he were interested.

Being interested in anything dealing with Billy the Kid, Chile, Charlie said, "I'm all ears."

Here is the story Herman told Chile Charlie about the short life of Billy the Kid:

Billy the Kid's real name was William Henry McCarty. When and where he was born or who his father was still unknown. He was estimated to be born in the 1860s, possibly in New York. History's first trace of the Kid as a youngster was in Indiana and then in Wichita, Kansas, in 1870. His mother, Catherine McCarthy, was a widow and single mother. He had a younger brother named Joseph.

On March 1, 1873, Catherine McCarthy married William Antrim in Santa Fe. Since there were now two Billys in the household, the Kid's mother called him by his middle name; he was now Henry McCarty-Antrim.

The family moved to Silver City in Grant County. Catherine's health deteriorated rapidly. She died of consumption on September 16, 1874.

The stepfather didn't want to be burdened with two small boys, so he separated them, placed them in foster homes, and left Silver City for Arizona. The Kid now had to earn his keep. He was put to work washing dishes and waiting tables at a restaurant. After a year of no parental guidance and looking out for himself, the Kid quickly fell in with the wrong crowd.

One of his troublemaking buddies, Sombrero Jack, stole some laundry from a Chinese laundry. Sombrero Jack told the Kid to hide the bundle. The Kid was caught with the laundry and was arrested. The county sheriff kept him locked up for a few days to scare him, but the Kid escaped and ran away.

The Kid fled to one of his foster families. They put him on a stagecoach to Clifton, Arizona, where his stepfather lived. But when he found his stepfather, Billy the Kid was disappointed to learn that his stepfather didn't want him and told the Kid to leave. All alone in a strange desert, the Kid wandered from one ranch to another to find work.

The Kid tramped around as a ranch hand and a gambler for the next two years. He then met up with a horse thief named John Mackey, who taught him the trade tricks of cattle rustling.

The two became partners. After some close calls, the Kid decided it was wiser to find a new occupation. He returned some stolen horses to the Army to clear himself and got to work as a ranch hand.

One day, while in a saloon in Camp Grant, Arizona, the Kid, age sixteen, got into serious trouble. He argued with a bully named Frank "Windy" Cahill, who had picked on him numerous times before. After some name-calling, Cahill rushed the Kid and slammed him down on the ground, then jumped on *top of him and slapped him in the face. The kid is hands-free to his revolver and fires it into Cahill's gut. When Cahill fell over, the Kid squirmed free, ran off, mounted the nearest horse, and fled Camp Grant.*

The Kid didn't want to be charged with murder; he left Arizona and returned to New Mexico. Now an outlaw and unable to find honest work, the Kid met up with another outlaw named Jesse Evans, the leader of a gang of cattle wrestlers called "The Boys." The gang went to Lincoln County, where "The Boys" joined forces with James Dolin. James was in a feud with an Englishman entrepreneur named John Tunstall and his attorney and partner Alex McSween. The feud would be famously known as the Lincoln County War.

The boys stole livestock, so arrests were made, and the Kid was eventually caught and placed in jail. Tunstall noticed something different about this rustler; he wasn't rough like the other men but just a boy who got a bad start in life and was looking for a place to belong. So, Tunstall gave him an ultimatum: if he testified against the other wrestlers, Tunstall would hire him as an employee. The Kid took Tunstall's offer.

Now fighting for Tunstall's side and hoping for a better future, the Kid changed his name to William H Bonney, but his friends still called him "Kid." Tensions were high, and the feud between the Dolans and Tunstall escalated to blood violence. John Tunstall was brutally murdered by members of Sheriff Brady's posse and "The Boys." Tunstall's ranch hands then formed a group called the "regulators." Now, the war was on.

At first, the deputized regulators tried to do things legally by serving warrants. Still, with the prejudiced Sheriff Brady and the biased court system, they couldn't count on justice being served. So, they took the law into their own hands. They retaliated by killing Bill Morton, Frank Baker, and William McCloskey. Then, they ambushed Sheriff Brady and his deputy George Henman in Lincoln. Last, they had a dramatic gunfight with Dolan's gunmen; Buckshot Rogers was killed.

The regulators' activities only made things worse. They were now viewed as bad guys. Warrants were put out for their arrest.

Now, Dolan's side struck back. Dolan's gunmen and newly appointed Sheriff, George Pippin, and his men had the McSween house surrounded by Alex McSween and many regulators trapped inside. Dolin sent for Col. Dudley at Fort Staunton for assistance. The Col. came with troops along with a howitzer and a Gatling gun. On the fifth day of the siege, the Dolan side was getting impatient, so they set the house on fire. By nightfall, the house was ablaze; the heat from the flames was overwhelming. The regulators panicked, so the coolheaded Billy the Kid, only about seventeen years old, took over the leadership.

The Kid divided the men into two groups. He led his party out the door first and ran in one direction to draw the line of fire towards them so McSween's party could make a run in the other direction and get away.

When the men ran out of the burning house, the Dolin side opened fire, and all hell broke loose. McSween and three men were killed, but Billy the Kid and others escaped into the darkness.

That activity ended the war, the regulators disbanded, and now Billy the Kid was a fugitive. He could not settle down. The Kid made his living by gambling and rustling cattle. The Kid heard of Gov. Axtell being replaced by Lou Wallace, who was now trying to bring law and order to Lincoln. The Kid wrote to the governor that he was tired of running and would surrender to authorities and testify against the Dolin side to have his murder charges dropped. The governor agreed and promised Billy the Kid a full pardon.

The Kid surrendered and testified in court, but the Santa Fe Ring influenced the court system, so members of the Dolin side, including James Dolin, were acquitted. Billy the Kid was in unfriendly territory. One of his threats was prosecutor attorney William Rynerson. He was part of the "Ring" and wanted to put the Kid on trial for the murder of Sheriff Brady. The Kid felt betrayed when he learned that Gov. Wallace didn't have the power to pardon him without Rynerson's cooperation, nor was the governor pressuring the attorney to collaborate. Wallace lost interest and left the Kid to his fate. Billy the Kid knew he didn't stand a chance in court. He lost faith in the governor, and he escaped jail.

On the run again, an outlaw, the Kid returned to making a living the only way he knew how-- rustling. New Mexico had other outlaws and rustlers, much worse than Billy the Kid. Still, the Kid gained fame again and was singled out by the newspaper that had built him up and made him something he wasn't. The newspaper had given him the name he would forever be known as Billy the Kid.

Since the Lincoln County War ended, the Kid spent the next two years eluding the law and living in and around Fort Sumner. While in Fort Sumner, he would kill a drunk at the saloon, but the killing was shrugged off and got almost no attention. Unfortunately, the kid got into more serious trouble, which earned him plenty of attention.

The trouble escalated when a posse from White Oaks surrounded Billy the Kid and his gang at a station house. During the standoff, the posse accidentally killed their deputy, James Carlisle. The death was accredited to Billy the Kid. It destroyed any chance of sympathy the public may have had for him. He did not think he would square things up with the governor and his pardon.

Pat Garrett was elected sheriff and then made a US Marshall, specifically to hunt for Billy the Kid.

Garrett was familiar with the Kid's habits and hideouts. Some thought that Garrett might have been a rustler himself or, at one time, had ridden with the Kid. While pursuing Billy the Kid, Garrett killed two of the Kid's closest friends. Finally, on December 23, 1880, Garrett trapped the Kid and three other gang members at a cabin in Stinking Springs. After a short standoff, Billy the Kid came out and surrendered.

He was quickly put on trial in Mesilla and was sentenced to hang for the murder of Sheriff Brady. After his sentence was passed, the Kid was taken to Lincoln, New Mexico, to await his hanging. The Kid was shackled and imprisoned in a room in the Lincoln Courthouse as two deputies took turns guarding him.

On April 28, 1881, the Kid made his most daring escape. He successfully got a drop on one of the lone guards by slipping his hand out of the handcuffs and using the heavy restraints to hit the deputy over the head. The Kid jerked the guard's pistol and told him to throw up his hands, but instead, the deputy ran.

The Kid had no choice but to shoot him. The other guard was across the street having dinner when he heard the gunshots. He ran toward the building. When Billy the Kid saw the guard approaching, he shot the guard with a shotgun. The Kid rode out of Lincoln a freeman and headed for the only place he could call home: Fort Sumner.

The Kid decided to lay low long enough that the law would give up hunting for him. He could rustle up some money and leave the territory.

By July of 1881, Garrett heard rumors that Billy the Kid was in the Fort Sumner area, so he rode out to the Fort Sumner area with two deputies.

On July 14, 1881, just before midnight, Pat Garrett waited until it was quiet before he slipped into Pete Maxwell's room and asked him about Billy the Kid. Garrett was a former employee of Mr. Maxwell. He might have tipped Garrett that the Kid was here.

At that exact moment, the Kid went to Maxwell's house with a knife to get some fresh beef for a late steak dinner. As he approached, he saw Garrett's two deputies on the porch. Since he didn't recognize a stranger, he cautiously entered Maxwell's room and asked Pete who those fellows were outside.

He got no answer; as the Kid walked towards the bed, he saw Garrett's silhouette, backed away, and asked in Spanish, " Who's there? Garrett recognized Billy's voice and fired his gun. The bullet pierced the Kid's heart; he fell to the floor. Garrett and Maxwell ran out of the room and huddled outside. The two deputies waited. They could hear the Kid gasping for breath; all was quiet.

Billy the Kid was dead. The next day, Billy the Kid was buried at Fort Sumner Cemetery near his two companions. He was killed not for who he was but for what people thought he was.

He was on the losing team. The Kid was made for other outlaws. Although he participated in killings, the men he fought against were much worse than he ever was. This 20-year-old lived a short life but made a lasting impression. With our attraction to Billy the Kid, the history of the Lincoln County Wars and its participants was remembered.

Thanks to Billy the Kid, New Mexico has a thriving tourism business with a steady flow of tourists each year who come to visit Billy the Kid sites. Even after the death, Billy the Kid is more likable; he has a large following worldwide. Billy the Kid is known as the Old West's favorite outlaw. (Information copied from the Internet.)

Now, would you like to visit his gravesite? Ask Herman Heppenstall.

"Of course," said Chile Charlie. The two men crossed the street and went to Billy the Kid's burial site. Chile Charlie saw the tombstone encased by solid steel bars to protect it from vandals and others who wanted to disgrace his tombstone.

Chile Charlie was delighted with the story of Billy the Kid. Charlie got into his El Camino and headed back to Las Cruces.

CHAPTER SIXTEEN

CHARLIE'S TRIP TO CLOUDCROFT

In late August, Chile Charlie opened the flap of his tent and scanned the surroundings until he located the community heat index thermometer. Despite being only ten o'clock, the thermometer displayed a scorching ninety-two degrees. The day promised to be exceptionally hot. Notably, Chile Charlie's tent was not air-conditioned or available throughout the City of Hope. What was he going to do?

He got out his trusty US Atlas and found some relief areas to visit. The possibilities included Ruidoso or Cloudcroft. The decision still needed to be made, but he gathered up his travel gear and put it in the back of his El Camino. He had his sleeping bag, tent, tools, Styrofoam icebox, gas can, and clothing.

At precisely eleven o'clock, Chile Charlie embarked on his journey in his reliable El Camino, heading towards White Sands. He stopped briefly at the visitor center's information kiosk at the White Sands National Park, took a moment at the restroom, and proceeded to Alamogordo. Eventually, a decision was made to make Cloudcroft his destination.

As he started up Route 82, Chile Charlie thought about the wonders of the great state of New Mexico. *"This landscape still speaks to the imagination of early days in the great Southwest. History lives in the rich cultural diversity that contributes its peculiar flavor to your mind. Over four hundred years ago, the conquistadors entered this* region reminiscent of parts of their native Spain. Since the sun shines daily, many outdoor activities await those living in this enchanted land. Every season features a variety of fun. Summer months offer activities that can be year-round in some parts of the state: camping, hiking, horseback riding, and fishing in state and national parks. Mountain climbing or river rafting invites the adventures of a lifetime. Swimming, golf, and tennis facilities can readily be throughout most city recreation departments and chambers of commerce. Cyclists will find plenty of opportunities for bicycling on the local side roads and designated bike trails.

"During winter, ten major critical areas in the state offered downhill skiing on various trails for the novice to the expert. Cross-country skiing, snowshoeing, snowmobiling, ice fishing, and skating are popular in some areas. New Mexico gives the hunter a variety of terrain and quarry."

Chile Charlie knows that many ghost towns that can be visited will allow you to poke around and taste what it was like during the 1880s. The Pueblo, Apache, and Navajo reservations draw people worldwide to observe the public celebrations and enjoy recreational opportunities. He continued to think about this as his El Camino labored to get up the mountainside.

As he reached the summit, he saw a sign that read 8705 feet elevation. He was now in Cloudcroft. Chile Charlie looked for the Chamber of Commerce or information center.

It was high noon, and the sun's rays beaned directly overhead, casting an intolerable white glow upon the roofs and streets of Cloudcroft. The drowsy town's adobe walls, spires, and sidewalks emitted heat in a quivering summer atmosphere. The leaves of the eucalyptus trees surrounding the Plaza stood motionless, limp, and relaxed under the scorching, searing blaze. The shadows of these trees add little shade. The sun was everywhere.

Charlie looked up and down Main Street, but no Chamber or information office sign existed. Finally, he saw a lonely soul who looked like she might help him. Sofia Hightower was a tall lady of about five foot eleven with bright eyes like those on one of the old-time automobiles. Her broad smile said, "How can I help you?"

Chile Charlie said, "You could help if you know where the Chamber office is in this wonderful village."

Sofia looked perplexed and answered, "The Chamber office is down the street on the second floor of the Sweeny Building. But there was not anyone employed as the director."

Chile Charles said, "That is not the answer I sought. I drove from Las Cruces to find out what made Cloudcroft tick."

Sofia explained, "I know somebody who could be of service in helping you learn more about the village. The village historian, Mr. Wentworth, would fit the bill perfectly."

Chile Charlie's eyes expanded, and they asked, "Where will I find this, Mr. Wentworth?"

Sofia said, "Mr. Wentworth has lunch daily at the Hinckley Inn just down the street. "I can take you there and introduce you if you wish?"

"That would be great," explained Chile Charlie. Off the two went to the Hinckley Inn to find Mr. Wentworth.

Sofia and Chile Charlie discovered Mr. Wentworth sitting in a back booth reading the local rag sheet all by his lonesome.

Sofia approached him and said, "Here is someone who wants to learn something about our community—Chile Charlie from Las Cruces." "Please meet Mr. Wentworth, our community's most knowledgeable historian."

"Gee, thanks, Sofia, for the introduction." Chile Charlie took a seat across from Mr. Wentworth. Charlie settled in for a Q&A session. Then Charlie asked softly, "How did Cloudcroft get its start?

Mr. Wentworth leaned back, cleared his throat, and said, "In the 1890s, the El Paso and Northern Railroad, organized by brothers Charles Bishop Eddy and John Arthur Eddy, arrived in the newly developed town of Alamogordo. The brothers intended to continue the rail line north to the mining town of White Oaks and beyond. This construction would require a steady supply of timber."

Mr. Wentworth drank coffee and continued his story, "In 1898, the Eddy brothers sent a survey crew into the Sacramento Mountains to determine the feasibility of extending a line up the summit. They wanted to harvest the trees. The team reported that not only was it possible, but the area could attract visitors.

"The name of Cloudcroft–a pasture for the clouds–was suggested, and work on the line soon began.

"By the end of the year, the rail line had been extended as far as Toboggan Canyon. The construction of a pavilion was started to accommodate the anticipated tourists. It consisted of a dining room, kitchen, parlor, entertainment hall, and forty tent sites on wooden platforms.

"In May 1899, the railroad reached Cox Canyon. In June 1899, the Pavilion (A cozy getaway place featuring knotty pine walls for a quaint yet

122

rustic setting) was formally opened by John Eddy. The first visitors rode the train as far as Toboggan and finished the journey by stagecoach," stated Mr. Wentworth.

Mr. Wentworth suddenly slid out of his seat and stretched. The move startled Chile Charlie. Even more so, Chile Charlie was taken aback when Wentworth said, "Waitress, waitress, bring us two pieces of your great apple pie and put some ice cream on them."

After receiving their apple pie, Mr. Wentworth continued his explanation of the beginning of Cloudcroft, "Favorable reports in newspapers quickly made Cloudcroft a popular destination. An additional resort, The Lodge, a hotel, was built as a more upscale alternative to The Pavilion. The rail line arrived in Cloudcroft in early 1900, and in June 1900, the train depot, located just west of The Pavilion, was finished. Meeting the trains became a daily activity in the village, with three arriving daily, bringing lumber, mail, and passengers."

Charlie said, "That's all fascinating, Mr. Wentworth, but is there anything new you can add to the history of Cloudcroft?"

Mr. Wentworth took a deep sigh, thought for a minute, and continued, "Well, in 1909, the Lodge burned down; it was rebuilt at its present location. All the construction was finished in 1911. The Pavilion also burned twice in the 1920s but was rebuilt each time to conform to the original plans.

"The Cloudcroft Lodge hosted numerous famous guests, including Judy Garland, Gilbert Roland, Clark Gable, and Pancho Villa. He was the Mexican general who invaded the United States. In the 1930s, the resort was managed by Conrad Hilton, who was born and raised in San Antonio, New Mexico. Hilton was familiar with The Lodge and wanted to be closer to his family as his hotel chain slowly climbed to prominence in the Southwest.

"As automobiles became popular, the rail line began to lose money. Passenger service ended in 1938. The last freight train ran in 1947. Since then, tourism has grown beyond The Lodge and Pavilion to Burro Street. Many small shops and restaurants are located there. In the summer, street dances are hosted. However, the town's population has not grown, remaining between 700 and 800 residents."

Wentworth continued his story by providing vital information about one landmark of Cloudcroft--the Trestle. He declared, "The Mexican Canyon Trestle is a recreated example of the now-defunct rail line that once ran up the mountain from Alamogordo to Cloudcroft. It is off Highway 82, less than one mile west of Cloudcroft.

"On Monday, December 13, 2010, a fire broke out in Cloudcroft. It destroyed two downtown buildings and caused smoke damage to several other businesses. The fire did considerable damage to the tourist attractions along Burro Street.

"The hundred-year-old Pine Stump Mall building, housing numerous businesses on the boardwalk, burned to the ground while the fire gutted the Copper Butterfly building. The building's walls were standing without a roof. Later that day, fire crews were forced to demolish the Copper Butterfly because of fire damage.

"Cloudcroft Mayor Dave Venable, owner of the Pine Stump Mall, reported that no one was injured in the fire. The buildings were unoccupied at the time of the blaze.

"The elimination of six businesses and related jobs just before Christmas was a severe economic loss to the community. Then, Mayor Venable revealed that New Mexico TV station KRQE first broke the story on Twitter. It quickly became the primary source of updates about the fire, including

Cloudcroft Webcam, which happened to be directed at Burro Avenue and the affected area.

"The cause of the fire was undetermined. A later investigation suggested that an electrical short, possibly related to holiday decorations, sparked the initial blaze."

Chile Charlie then thanked Mr. Wentworth for all this information. It's hard to digest it all at one time. Chile Charlie inquired, "If it's okay with you, Mr. Wentworth, let's meet again tomorrow at the **Hinckley** Inn and continue our discussion about the people who reside in this fair village?"

Mr. Wentworth said honestly, "That would be an excellent idea. I will see you tomorrow. We will talk about the people that reside in Cloudcroft."

Chile Charlie asked Sofia for directions to the nearest campsite area. Once he arrived, he set up his tent and got some of his vittles for supper. He ate with vigor and gave much thought to what Mr.

Wentworth had been telling him about the debut and history of Cloudcroft.

The following day, Charlie got up revitalized. He struggled out of his bedroll, stretched, and breathed in the fresh air of the mountains. He could hardly wait to talk to Mr. Wentworth again, but he had several hours of wait before joining Mr. Wentworth at the **Hinckley** Inn. *"What in the world would he do?"* he thought.

Charlie elected that he would mosey around the community and look at the architecture of the houses and the businesses. What he saw was a mixture of old and new structures. Some structures hadn't seen a coat of paint in the last fifty years, while others were spotlessly clean and looked brand-new. Charlie asked himself why this was. Wasn't there any civic pride within the community that would let some of the structures look like they needed to be torn down or replaced? He thought he might ask Mr. Wentworth his opinion when he met him later. It was now 11:30, and off he went to the Hinckley Inn to see Mr. Wentworth.

When Chile Charlie arrived at the café, he found Mr. Wentworth and a stranger sitting in the booth near the back of the cafeteria. Chile Charlie said hello to Mr. Wentworth.

Mr. Wentworth told Chile Charlie, "I want you to meet Dr. Henry Aguilar. Dr. Aguilar is a New Mexico State University professor knowledgeable about the families living in Cloudcroft."

"I hope you don't mind if Dr. Aguilar sits in on our discussion about the population in Cloudcroft." Chile Charlie acknowledged it would be no problem if Dr. Aguilar added information about the community population's makeup.

Then Charlie asked if you two gentlemen wanted to order coffee with the apple pie they had ordered. Mr. Wentworth and Dr. Aguilar thought it was an excellent idea and placed the order with the waitress.

Chile Charlie questioned Dr. Agular about the general breakdown of the village's population. Dr. Agular stated the statistics from the 2000 Census by saying, "There were 749 people, 320 households, and 224 families residing in the village. Dr. Agular concluded from all these statistics that Cloudcroft was not an affluent community by any stretch of the imagination."

Mr. Wentworth took over the conversation by stating, "Cloudcroft is home to three festivals, each taking place at Zenith Park. Local and regional artists sell their arts and crafts items. Live music and entertainment are provided. Local churches and civic organizations hold activities and competitions.

"The May Fair is the kickoff of the summer tourist season on Memorial Day Weekend. Following the 4th of July, the July Jamboree is the smallest and newest of the three festivals. In October, the third and final event, Oktoberfest, is celebrated. It has an autumn atmosphere with the local aspen groves turning golden rather than a traditional German Oktoberfest. It is the final outdoor event before the winter snow and the close of the traditional tourist season. Mr. Wentworth was enormously proud of these events and pointed to the bulletin board displaying the next event."

Chile Charlie inquired about the tale of the local Lodge's ghost---"Rebecca." Both Wentworth and Agular talked simultaneously about this famous story. Finally, Mr. Wentworth prevailed by giving Chile Charlie his recollection of the tale. He said, "There is a popular legend at The Lodge that dates to the early 1900s.

"The story involves a beautiful young chambermaid with striking blue eyes and shocking red hair. She disappeared from her quarters after her lumberjack lover found her in the arms of another."

Wentworth continued his story, "Although we might not have seen her, there are those who vow that Rebecca still wanders the halls of this historic hotel. It has been said that ashtrays have been seen sliding across tables unassisted, doors open and closed for no apparent reason, furniture has been moved, lights have turned on and off by themselves, and fires have spontaneously ignited in the fireplace, among other unexplained incidents that occur to this day. Guests and employees continue to relate odd incidents attributed to Rebecca's spirit. However, none of them are threatening or frightening, but more of a fun and playful nature. Some believe Rebecca is searching for a new lover or friend who might appreciate her flirtatious and mischievous ways."

Dr. Agular concluded the tale by saying, "Take a close look at the portrait of Rebecca in the Lounge. Who knows, you will be the one to see her. And if you meet her, tell her we were fond enough of her to name the restaurant in her honor."

Chile Charlie turned to the two gentlemen and explained that he now gathered a great deal of understanding about what makes the village of Cloudcroft tick. This story has all the makings of a jewel to be discovered, making Cloudcroft tick that.

He then suggested that they dine on the cuisine of Hinckley Inn. Mr. Wentworth and Dr. Aguilar agreed that the witching hour of lunch was upon them, and they should place their lunch order.

After lunch, Chile Charlie returned to his El Camino, packed his notes and belongings, and started towards Las Cruces. As he descended the mountain, he couldn't help but reflect on the twists and turns of his journey. The change of scenery mirrored the unpredictability of life itself. Despite the unexpected return to the day's heat, he realized that every journey, like the fluctuating temperature, brings challenges and rewards. With a renewed sense of resilience, Charlie continued his drive towards Las Cruces, ready for whatever lay ahead on the winding road of his adventures.

CHAPTER SEVENTEEN

CHILE CHARLIE FINDS MOGOLLON

The day was fall-like. The thermometer read an incredible seventy-three degrees. Chile Charlie was happy as a man in an ice cream store with a sign that read, "Eat all you can free of charge." He stepped out of his tent, stretched, and considered visiting the Camp Hope Director this morning. He met a sweet voice that rang like a church chime as he walked to the head office area.

Ruby Hathaway, who owned the voice, said, "What are you up to this fine fall morning, Charlie?" Ruby Hathaway had long passed the boom of youth, but there was still something about her. She was a middle-aged queen who ruled Camp Hope with an iron fist. She had been married to a man who put

Camp Hope together. Camp Hope was a designated place where many homeless individuals could set up housekeeping away from the community.

"Ruby, I am interested in finding information about some of the long-lost mining towns in New Mexico." "Where do you suggest I start looking?"

Hathaway didn't hesitate. She said, "Charlie, you should go to Branigan Library and see the noted Southwest historian Christina Doodd.

Charlie thanked Ruby and left for the library. It took him forty-five minutes to walk to the Branigan Library.

This was the first time that Charlie was in the library. He decided to obtain a library card before talking to Ms. Doodd.

After Charlie got his library card, he introduced himself to Ms. Doodd's office.

"How may I help you, Mr. Chile Charlie," asked Ms. Doodd.

"I understand you are an expert on abandoned mining towns in New Mexico, and I would like some directions to one I could visit soon," Charlie said.

Ms. Doodd stated, "Yes, some considered me an expert in abandoned mining towns in New Mexico. I would be more than delighted to help."

"She suggests you travel to Mogollon, a small village only three and a half hours' drive. It will offer you a wonderful experience."

Chile Charlie asked, "Is there a person he should contact to provide him with information regarding the village's history, culture, and noteworthy happenings, and the best way to get to Mogollon?

Ms. Doodd answered, "The best way to Mogollon is to take Inter-State 10 to Deming, turn north on State Route 180 to Silver City (watch for the fork), and continue north on Route 180 to the Mogollon exit. There will be a dirt road, which is very bumpy for about ten miles. When you arrive, Charlie, look for Stuart Fizzell. He is the local historian who can provide the information you desire."

With that information, Charlie said his goodbyes to Ms. Doodd and returned to Camp Hope. During his walk back, he processed as much of the material he received as he could.

Chile Charlie packed up his El Camino and departed for Silver City. The trip would take him about two hours and arrive at about four o'clock. He decided to stay overnight in Silver City and proceed to the Village of Mogollon the following day.

He had read that Silver City had a gelato establishment. That sparked his interest in discovering what gelato was all about. The establishment's name was <u>A Lotta of Gelato</u>. He found it was Italian ice cream.

He ordered a raspberry sundae to eat before he struck camp for the night. There was a lovely campsite just north of the city. He pitched his tent and set out to cook ham, beans, and rice.

After a good night's sleep, Chile Charlie broke camp and reloaded his El Camino quickly, and he drove north. After thirty minutes, he saw the turn-off to Mogollon.

The dirt road was bumpy and needed better maintenance. It took another thirty minutes to travel fifteen miles to the village. By this time, he was tired of being jostled by the rough road, so he pulled over to the side of the road and took a brief break. He looked around and saw a beautiful vista that would take your breath away in a New York minute.

After admiring the pleasing vista, Charlie drove to the center of Mogollon. He spotted the tourist center office, parked his vehicle, and entered the building. He asked to speak to Mr. Stuart Fizzell. The man behind the desk stated, "I am Stuart Fizzell; what can I do you for?"

Mr. Stuart Fizzell had the look of a prospector of the 1860s. He was tall and gangly and wore a clean set of bib overalls. His face was filled with gorge-looking wrinkles. His hands were gnarled from years of shoveling and picking. He wore logger boots that reached way above his ankles. His character was cheerful, and his outlook on life was positive. Few people would have guessed that he would have a doctorate in geology.

"My name is Chile Charlie from Las Cruces, and I would like to learn some of the history, culture, and what makes Mogollon tick."

"Glad to meet you, Charlie," answered Stuart. "Would you like some mountain-brewed java, Charlie?"

"Of course, that would be very hospitable of you, Stuart," Charlie responded.

Stuart left and returned with a large cup of steaming coffee. Charlie grabbed the mug and took a small sip of his coffee. Chile Charlie exclaimed, "Wow, this is the best coffee I've had in a long time. Can we start with the history of the Village of Mogollon?"

"Yes, the historical background of Mogollon is fascinating. It is also called the Mogollon Historic District, a former mining town in the Mogollon Mountains in Catron County, New Mexico. It was founded in the 1880s at the bottom of Silver Creek

Canyon to support the gold and silver mines in the surrounding mountains.

"The "Little Fannie mine" became the most important employer for the town. During the 1890s, Mogollon had a transient population of 3,000 and 6,000 miners. Because of its isolation, it had a reputation as one of the wildest mining towns in the West. Today, Mogollon is listed as the Fannie Hill Mill and Company Town Historic District on the National Register of Historic Places.

"In the middle 1870s, Sergeant James C. Cooney of Fort Bayard found a rich strand of gold in the Gila Mountains near the future site of Mogollon. A miner named John Eberle built the first cabin in Mogollon in 1889 after mines were developed in Silver Creek, which runs through the town. A jail and post office opened in 1890, and the first school was added in 1892 during this period of growth.

"The Little Fanny was an exceptionally dusty mine. *Miner's consumption,* a series of ailments affecting miners, caused miners to work at Little Fanny for three years or less. In response, the owners developed a method of spraying water from the jackhammers as they broke the quartz for removal, thus reducing airborne dust. In 1909, the population of Mogollon was 2,000.

"Mogollon absorbed the population of nearby Cooney and helped towns like Glenwood, Gila, and Cliff grow because of their locations along the trail to Mogollon. Between 1872 and 1873, the stagecoach from Mogollon to Silver City was robbed twenty-three times by the same assailant. Agents of Wells Fargo eventually apprehended him.

"That same year, the town had five saloons, two restaurants, four merchandise stores, two hotels, and several brothels in two red-light districts. The town also had a photographer, the Midway Theatre, an ice maker, and a bakery."

Chile Charlie interrupted Mr. Fizzell and asked him if there was more coffee. Mr. Fizzell answered, "Yes, just give me a minute, and I will get some for you."

"Thank you," said Chile Charlie. Stuart returned with another large cup of coffee.

Then Charlie said," Please continue."

Stuart Fizzell stated, "The Silver City and Mogollon Stage Line provided daily service, hauling passengers, freight, gold, and silver bullion eighty miles between the two towns. The trip took almost fifteen hours."

Chile Charlie was surprised when Mr. Fizzell stated, "By 1915, payroll in Mogollon was $75,000 monthly. The community expanded to 1,500 that year, with electricity, water, and telephone facilities.

143

The school offered education to three hundred students.

"From early in its life, Mogollon was plagued by fires and floods. The first big fire of 1894 wiped out most of the town buildings made of wood. Fires followed in 1904, 1910, 1915, and 1942. Citizens usually immediately rebuilt, each time using more stone and adobe. Floods rushed through Silver Creek in 1894, 1896, 1899, and 1914. The floods washed away mine tailings, dumps, bridges, houses, and people.

"During WW I, the demand for gold and silver dropped, and many of Mogollon's mines shut down. The population in 1930 had fallen to a reported two hundred. The town grew again during a short resurgence in gold value during the late 1930s. Still, during World War II, it shrank again, never recovering its stature.

"Several mines were built in the Mogollon area, including the Little Fanny, Champion, McKinley, Pacific, and Deadwood. With older prospectors, minors extracted approximately $1.5 million of gold and silver in 1913, forty percent of New Mexico's precious metals for that year.

"Over 18 million ounces of silver were taken from the mines of the Mogollon Mountains, which was one-quarter of New Mexico's total production. Close to Twenty million dollars in gold and silver were extracted, with silver accounting for about two-thirds of the total. The entire Mogollon community was added to the National Register of Historic Places as Fannie Hill Mill and Company Town Historic District in 1987. It was cited for its industrial and architectural legacy from 1875 through 1949."

Chile Charlie interrupted Mr. Fizzell again. "Are there any cultural activities outside of the confines of Mogollon that would shed more light on the village? What made it tick?"

Mr. Fizzell answered, "In 1973, a spaghetti western, *My Name is Nobody*, starring Henry Fonda and Terence Hill, was filmed here. A saloon and general store in town were built as part of the movie set, and today, the town is privately owned.

"The town is the location of several small businesses, including the Silver Creek Inn, which operates in a former boarding lodge called the Mogollon House, built by Frank Lauderbaugh in 1885. The establishment is filled with ghosts from the mining era. Many regarded Silver City as merely a railhead for Mogollon's eight-team freight wagons packed with gold and silver ore.

"With the decline in precious metal values after World War I, operating the mines was no longer profitable. However, the town grew after a brief recovery in gold prices in 1937.

"However, WW II caused a slash in demand for precious metals. The devastating fire of 1942 almost finished the town. In 1952, the Little Fanny was the only mine in operation. Today, it is silent. When the Little Fanny mine closed, Mogollon deteriorated."

There was a knock on the front door, and in stepped a strange character. Mr. Fizzell said, "Hello, Sadie, you are in time to meet Chile Charlie from Las Cruces. He is here to learn about the history and culture of our small village."

"Great," said Sadie Hopkins. Sadie, storyteller personified, dressed in a Victorian-style outfit: dark stockings, ankle-length skirts with petticoats, and a white shirt. She wore her hair swept up in a bun like most women in the town. She was as short as a pet horse; her face was round like a small ball. But her footwear was Niki-made tennis shoes.

Stuart said, "Ms. Hopkins is one of the famous storytelling guides in Mogollon. She tours the downtown and relates stories of the past."

Charlie asked, "Sadie, give me an example of a story you tell people. Sadie pulled up close to Chile Charlie and said softly, "Did you know that Billy the Kid had a sweet tooth for one of our early business ladies here?"

'No," said Charlie, "Tell me the details, please."

Sadie swung around so the backrest was in front of her and she could lean on it for support. She told her story in the best storytelling voice.

"You have heard of the Dolan/Sweeney feud in Sierra County. Still, "Did you hear of the Edwards/Milken feud and Catron County? Little-known William Monty was a ranch hand on the Edwards ranch; James Milken ran a mercantile store monopoly in Catron County. Ben Edwards opened a competitive store when Edwards was murdered. This activity set off another feud.

"Now, Billy the Kid sometimes used the ranch as a sanctuary. He rustled cattle and stole horses, so he occasionally needed a hideaway from the law.

"When Sally Summers met Billy, they became instant friends. Stories say every cowboy in Catron County loved her, but Billy held a special place for her. The two would often sit on the ranch house porch and talk well into the night. They also went on long rides together, racing one another.

"Billy was an impulsive and adventurous young man, but I'd never wager against Sally instigating the races.

"Sally said Billy was the pink of politeness... as courteous a little gentleman as I ever met." He was a year younger and may have been in love with Sally, but she was smart enough to know nothing good could ever come of a union with the wrong boy. And she was right.

"Sally lived in Mogollon for thirty years. She rode in the Old Timer's Parades. Unlike the Cowboys, she rode sidesaddle as was her custom, wearing her old-fashioned riding habit. She rode straight and tall, commensurate with the pillar of the community she had become.

"Her accomplishments as an entrepreneur, developer, and woman led her to be known as the First Lady of Mogollon," That is the story of Sallie Summers.

With those words, Sadie got up and left without another word. Chile Charlie was left with multiple thoughts of what would come next from this little village.

After having lunch, Chile Charlie returned to his El Camino, gathered his notes, and started towards Las Cruces. He was captivated by the shift in scenery and the temperature change.

CHAPTER EIGHTEEN

CHARLIE'S TRIP TO HILLSBORO

After Chile Charlie's expedition to Mogollon, New Mexico, he looked for another vanished mining village whose hay day had passed. The Atlas was stored in the glove compartment. He pulled it out and looked for a small village off the beaten path. His eyes focused on Hillsboro. Interestingly, Chile Charlie had experience with the name Hillsboro in Illinois. But this was Hillsboro, New Mexico. He just had to get there within the next few days.

Chile Charlie thought it would be essential to research Hillsboro before visiting. He put on his walking shoes and rushed over to the Branigan Library. He asked the research librarian if there were any books or materials about Hillsboro, New Mexico.

She softly said, "Yes, some books in the reference library have information about that small village. We can gather those books for your examination and study if you follow me."

After two hours of exhausting study, Chile Charlie thought he had enough background information to make the excursion to Hillsboro.

He drove north on Interstate 25. He saw the most beautiful light blue sky that any artist would pay a million dollars to capture on canvas as he was going. He noticed what he thought was an Aplomb Falcon high above him. Now, this was a mystery to him. Aplomb Falcons rarely migrate this far north from their natural habitat in the Chiricahua Mountains, about one hundred miles south. Chile Charlie stopped his daydreaming when he saw the turnoff sign for Kingston. He turned west. He was headed for the Black Range Mountains, which Hillsboro used as its mystic.

After thirty minutes, Chile Charlie found himself on the outskirts of Hillsboro. The roadway through Hillsboro was also its Main Street. Many small towns were created similarly at the turn of the century. The businesses were always looking for pass-through traffic that would help them maintain a profit. The buildings on each side of the road look like they would've been a saloon, a bank, a church, a grocery store, and even a hotel during Hillsboro's earlier days.

He drove about ten miles an hour. He looked to the right and left. He saw dirt roads leading to the few remaining buildings that may have been company housing years ago. He sought someone to inform him about this small community's history, culture, and background. There was no one in sight-- no one was on the streets. He looked hard for anyone to tell him about Hillsboro.

Fifteen minutes later, Chile Charlie spotted a man. The man had not shaved for several days, and his face and hands were covered with grime. His shoes were torn, and his coat, several sizes too small, hung tightly on his body. The man looked like he had come out of an old-time movie. His eyes were clear, and he looked straight ahead as he walked rapidly later. He was tall; his coat was too small, emphasizing that impression. He was carrying a book under his left arm, and a small terrier dog ran at his heels.

He calls to him to stop and talk. Charlie introduced himself.

Charlie said, "To whom do I have the pleasure of talking?"

The man looked preoccupied but said, "My name is Chester Woodford. "I am on my way to my galley, but you can tag along if you wish."

Chile Charlie asked, "How long have you lived in Hillsboro?"

"All my life."

Chile Charlie said, "Then you know the history and background of Hillsboro. Is that right?"

"Yes, I have a background, and I can talk to you about it if you wish." The conversation about the history and background of Hillsboro was on its way.

Mr. Woodford said, "Hillsboro is a small, unincorporated community in Sierra County, New Mexico, founded in 1877 following the discovery of gold. The community was the county seat of Sierra County from 1884 until 1936.

Hot Springs became the county seat. Later, Hot Springs changed its name to Truth or Consequences. Hillsboro served as the Sierra County seat of government from these territory days until 1936. The celebrated courthouse was sold in 1939 and partially dismantled. Still, Hillsboro survived, buoyed by gold and surrounded by cattle ranches. The remains of Hillsboro's majestic courthouse and jail still stand against the backdrop of the magnificent Black Range Mountains.

"The prospectors named the town Hillsborough in December 1877, but later shortened to Hillsboro. By 1880, the town had four companies of soldiers and four hundred miners, but the population soon grew to seven hundred. A county courthouse was built in 1892. By 1907, the population was 1200. A June 10, 1914 flood caused considerable damage to many town buildings."

After drinking water, Chester picked up his story, "The first house was built in August 1877. Two prospectors, Dan Dugan and Dave Stitzel, found loose pieces of rock (float is the geologic term) that assayed at $160 per ton in gold and silver. The area was the future Opportunity Mine. Soon, ore was discovered at the nearby Rattlesnake vein (geology) by Dugan and Frank Pitcher. A placer deposit of gold was found in November at the Rattlesnake and Wicks gulches.

"Ore was pulverized with arrestees in Hillsboro, including a 10-stamp mill built in 1878." Writer's note: (A stamp mail is a milling machine that crushes material by pounding rather than grinding.)"

Chile Charlie excitedly interrupted Chester, saying, "That information is certainly interesting, and I can use most of it in my writing."

"Would you like to continue your story, Chester?"

Chester continued, "From 1911 to 1931, total production of gold ore was 836 tons, gold-copper-silver ore was 5,470 tons, and copper ore was 200 tons.

"Now, it was reported that the ore deposits of the Hillsboro or Las Animas mining district were four general types: (1) fissure veins in andesite flows, (2) disseminated deposits in monzonite porphyry, replacement deposits in limestone, and placer gold deposits, Chester said without letting Chile Charlie interrupt him again. Chester was on a roll.

He continued, "The Copper Flat volcano to the northeast of Hillsboro is the source of the gold in the area. The four-mile-wide volcano is characterized by a Cretaceous quartz monzonite stock within a topographic depression. Surrounded by surface andesite flows over two thousand feet thick, the radial quartz latite or rhyolite dikes were everywhere. The stock generated the porphyry copper deposits, gold-bearing veins, and gold placers. About twenty-six major veins are forming a radial pattern from the stock. The Gold Dust Camp placer deposits are found in the alluvium of the dry gulches radiating off Copper Flat, and the andesite flows. The fissure veins produced 51,000 ounces of gold, while the placer deposits produced 110,000 ounces."

Mr. Woodford stopped momentarily and continued his story, "The Sternberg Mine at Copper Flat produced two hundred tons of copper ore between 1911 and 1934. By 1959, Bear Creek Mining Company had discovered a mineralized breccia pipe within the stock. Quintana Minerals Corporation started open-pit mining in 1980. The ore averaged 0.45 percent copper. Ore minerals included pyrite, chalcopyrite, sphalerite, and galena."

Chile Charlie spoke quietly, "Wow, all that information about how Hillsboro was the center of ore mining at the turn of the century was impressive to me." "Did Hillsboro have any other notable people or events I could use in my description?"

Chester was silent for a few minutes. He turned to Charlie and said, "Mr. Crews, a physician and American Civil War veteran, had resided here for several years. Frank W. Parker, a future New Mexico Supreme Court Justice, was born here. Mr.

Parker presided over the famous murder trial of Albert J. Fountain."

(Writer's note: The disappearance and murder of Albert J. Fountain was found in Wikipedia.)

"On February 1, 1896, Fountain and his eight-year-old son Henry disappeared near White Sands on the way to their home in Mesilla. They returned from Lincoln, New Mexico, where Fountain assisted the prosecution in bringing charges against Oliver M. Lee and William McNew. All that was found at the disappearance site were Fountain's buckboard wagon, several empty cartridge cases, cravat and papers, and two pools of blood. The only sign of Henry Fountain was a blood-soaked handkerchief with two powder-blackened coins, the handkerchief still carefully knotted in one corner. Missing were the victims' bodies, a blanket, a quilt, and Fountain's Winchester rifle.

"Some people speculated that 'Black JackKetchum' and his gang were involved. Most were convinced the disappearances could be attributed to Lee, a noted rancher, land developer, and a part-time Deputy U.S. Marshal. Lee's employees, Jim Gilliland and William McNew, were also suspected of involvement. Lee and Gilliland were pursued by lawman Pat Garrett and a posse, who engaged them in a gunfight near Alamogordo. However, after Deputy Sheriff Kent Kearney was mortally wounded on July 12, 1898, Garrett and his posse withdrew. Lee and Gilliland later negotiated their surrender to others. They were defended by Albert Bacon Fall, who later would become the first United States presidential cabinet member convicted of a felony and sentenced to prison during the Teapot Dome Scandal. The accused were acquitted due to a lack of evidence.

Albert Fountain was a powerful rival to landowners Fall and Lee. Fall was also known to hate Fountain as a political rival, just as Fountain hated

Fall. Fall's association with Lee began when he had defended Lee in a criminal case. Mr. Fountain had repeatedly challenged Fall and his men in the courts and the political arena.

"As the bodies of Fountain and his son were never found, the prosecution was greatly hampered. No one was ever charged with the murder of Albert Fountain. Lee and his employees, McNew and Gilliland, were tried for the murder of Henry Fountain. Charges also were never filed for the death of Deputy Sheriff Kearney. The charges against McNew were dismissed, while Lee and Gilliland were acquitted.

Memorials to Albert Jennings Fountain and his son are in the Masonic Cemetery in Las Cruces. However, their actual burial site remains a mystery.

"I am sure there are more, but I cannot recall them right now for my life," answered Chester.

"But you know Hillsboro was in Eugene Manlove Rhodes' 1920 novel <u>Stepsons of Light,</u> and 1986, Lewis *& Clark & George* was filmed here," Chester said.

Chile Charlie became restless and proclaimed that the information about the past was fascinating. But what are you doing in Hillsboro now to bring back some of the hay days and the vitality that Hillsboro's history provided?

"Charlie, I am so glad you asked that question.

"If you have time, I will ask Abigail Anderson to join us for coffee. She can describe what we're trying to provide as a tourist distraction here in Hillsboro."

In less than fifteen minutes, Abigail walked in. She was a tall, shapely young lady with a smile that filled the bottom part of her face. She was dressed in a royal blue pantsuit tailored to her body.

"Abigail, I want you to meet Chile Charlie from Las Cruces. He is writing a story about our community, and he would like to know what we're doing to improve the prosperity of our former mining village. Can you help us," asked Chester.

Ms. Anderson answered in the affirmative. She started her dialogue about what the leaders of Hillsboro have done and are planning to make Hillsboro a tourist destination. Abigail rambled off the following description of the progress in attracting tourists to Hillsboro like a pre-recorded message.

"Hillsboro's walkable "downtown" invites visitors to soak up the adobe ambiance of the historic homes, churches, and the Black Range Museum. Two popular cafes dish up flavorful home-cooked fare while locals discuss the latest news. You'll find antiques, art, books, photographs, and pottery produced locally and New Mexico wines served at the Vintage Wines Shop.

"On the south hill, the Hillsboro Community Center hosts concerts, dances, films, and theatre; the library offers free Wi-Fi. Every Friday evening, local musicians gather for the acoustic "picking circle." They take turns sharing songs and the fun of music-making, and drop-ins are welcome.

"Annual Hillsboro events include the Zia Velo bicycle race in March and Christmas in the Foothills on the first Saturday in December. Over the Labor Day weekend, the Hillsboro Historical Society is producing a dramatization of a notorious murder trial held in Hillsboro in 1896.

"In 1892, Hillsboro built a handsome brick courthouse on the frontier to symbolize civilization. The courthouse was chosen for the politically charged trial of rancher Oliver Lee and two cowhands for the murder of Judge Albert Jennings Fountain and his eight-year-old son Henry. They disappeared on a lonely stretch of desert between Lincoln and Mesilla in 1894.

"The trial reads like a who's who of 1890's New Mexico territory: Sherriff Pat Garrett, the arresting officer; Albert Bacon Fall, defense attorney; and Thomas Catron, prosecuting. Telegraph lines were strung twenty miles from Lake Valley to Hillsboro for the occasion, and reporters transmitted the trial proceedings to the Wall Street Journal in New York City.

"In the absence of bodies, the case against Oliver Lee and his men couldn't be proved, and the jury's verdict was "Not guilty. This notorious trial put Hillsboro on the map. Yet, the alleged crime was so distasteful that it was said to have delayed the statehood of New Mexico for over a decade.

"The Hillsboro Apple Festival put Hillsboro on the map. The festival grew out of a holiday weekend sidewalk sale that started in the early 1960s. It was going gangbuster for many years, but now Labor Day is just spread too thin for visitors," Abigail said.

"The Harvest Wine Festival in Las Cruces and the Hatch Chile Festival became too much completion for our event. We had to drop it."

"Thank you, Abigail, for the most interesting update on how you have changed the downtown area of Hillsboro. There is no question that you have put in the assets needed to improve this formerly important mining community. But now the question is, what will you do to entice tourists to come here? And spend money and spread the word about what this wonderful community is all about," asked Chile Charlie.

Abigail answered, "We use the Internet. We have a wonderful website partnering with the New Mexico Department of Tourism. And any other means that would be inexpensive for us to advertise. Our best methodology will be that of word-of-mouth advertising."

"Thank you both for such a valuable lesson about the rise and fall of this wonderful community of Hillsboro. I look forward to telling your story to the world," revealed Chile Charlie."

"I've got to get back to Las Cruces before it gets too dark to drive safely," uttered Charlie.

CHAPTER NINETEEN

CHILE CHARLE IN KINGSTON

It was a crisp and spicy morning in early October when Chile Charlie arose from a good night's sleep. The lilacs and the laburnums with the glory fires of autumn hung, burning and slashing in the air.

The rare larch trees and the pomegranates flung their purple and yellow flames in brilliant, broad splashes along the slanting sweep of the Las Cruces area woodlands. The sensual fragrance of an ordinary innumerable deciduous flower rose upon the swooning atmosphere. Everywhere Charlie looks, he sees brooded stillness, serenity, and the peace of God.

However, the need to travel swept into Chile Charlie's mind. But where to go was his hesitation. He had already been to so many villages and towns. Charlie scanned his Atlas. There were so many small places from which to choose.

Chile Charlie thought that it would help to explore Kingston. He had been to Hillsboro, about seven miles east of Kingston, and could compare these two communities. They may have had a similar history.

Charlie dressed in his usual southwest attire: a red checkered shirt, clean straight-legged Levis, white Stetson hat, and roper boots. He put his tape recorder in his pocket as he headed for his El Camino vehicle.

Charlie filled his tank at the Shell Convenience store, paid his gas bill, and drove to the I-25 North ramp. He was on his way to explore Kingston, New Mexico.

At the turnoff, Charlie turned west. He traveled through Hillsboro and then arrived in Kingston. There was no hustle and bustle on the streets, just the quiet solitude of a small town once busy and thriving. Charlie sought someone to give him information about Kingston's history and culture.

He spotted a building with a Kingston Museum sign in the front yard. He introduced himself to the lady sitting behind a small wooden desk. Chile Charlie said, "My name is Chile Charlie. I am from Las Cruces. I am compiling information about abandoned mining towns in the southwestern part of New Mexico. You could say I'm a 'pocket writer' or a bum looking for a free meal."

The lady replied, "I am Juanita Checker. I have operated this museum as a tourist attraction for ten years. I know some of Kingston's histories and would happily share what I know."

Charlie looked at her. He saw a round-faced woman with a plump body to go with the face and what he thought had not had a prosperous lifestyle, but that did not let her hold back from being friendly and helpful to others.

Ms. Checker said, "I have some hot coffee I could share with you if you'd like Chile Charlie?"

"OK," Charlie answered. Juanita left the room to get each a cup of black coffee. Upon her return, she directed Chile Charlie to the far end of the museum, a couch, and a recliner chair. The late-morning sun rays filtered through the large bay window at the room's rear, providing warmth and light that Charlie and Juanita welcomed.

They sat so they could see each other. After two sips of coffee, Juanita began talking about her favorite subject — the history of Kingston.

In her soft and teacher-like voice, Juanita said, "The village of Kingston is in Sierra County. The present population is thirty-two. The community is in the Black Range Mountain area along New Mexico State Road 152.

"In 1882, Kingston was established following the discovery of a substantial silver ore deposit by miner Jack Sheddon. The region saw a rapid number of mines developing, with the Iron King Mine being one of them and subsequently lending its name to the town.

"Originally, Kingston was called Percha City, which translates to hanger; Kingston was surveyed the same year. Soon, the population grew to over 1800. With the Depression of 1893, the mining activities in the area were drastically curtailed. Then, during World War II, there was a brief resurgence of silver mining. But by 1952, most production was over.

"The Iron King, Empire, and Brush Heap were some of the first three mines in the area. Most of the production was within 460 feet of the surface. This was called the supergene zone, where oxidation of ore occurs. The Lady Franklin Mine was the largest producer of high-grade silver from 1880 to 1893, averaging fifteen ounces per ton."

Then, shifting gears, Juanita said, "Kingston became a thriving metropolis overnight and soon offered all the trappings of civilization and culture. At the height of its silver mining boom, the population of Kingston topped 7,000, outstripping Albuquerque by at least 1,000 people. Numerous hotels played host to Mark Twain, Butch Cassidy, the Sundance Kid, Black Jack Ketchum, and of course Billy the Kid.

"There were several stage lines that served all the major routes. Kingston supported twenty-three saloons that advertised fresh oysters twenty-four hours a day. The town had fourteen grocery and general merchandise stores, a brewery, three newspapers, and an Opera House where the famous Lillian Russell Troup once performed.

"The Percha Bank was built in 1884 and was the largest bank in the biggest city in the New Mexico Territory."

"Wow, what an amazing story you weaved about the beginning of Kingston. What happened that the city declined," Chile Charlie questioned.

Juanita said, "It is incredible but true. It all ended as quickly as it had begun. The silver panic of 1893 and the establishment of the new gold standard dropped silver prices by ninety percent. With the mines playing out and profits becoming losses, the town began to fold.

"Most residents left, tearing down buildings for materials to be used elsewhere. The Percha Bank, once the home to seven million dollars in silver mining in the area, closed its building and moved the offices to neighboring Hillsboro to support the gold mines there.

"Today, only a few buildings remain from those glory days of over a century ago. The old Assay Office has been renovated as a private residence. The Victoria Hotel partially burned in the

'30s and is now a private residence. The Black Range Lodge, open as a Bed and breakfast, was constructed from the ruins of Pretty Sam's Casino across the street," Ms. Checker lamented.

"The Percha Bank building served for years as a Post Office and a storage area for mining equipment. Today, the Percha Bank building is the only fully intact original structure in the town, complete with its ornate lobby, teller windows, and classic old-west bank vault, once home to so much wealth."

"Ms. Checker, the background and the pictures were fascinating to me, but what does the future have in store for Kingston," asks Chile Charlie.

Juanita looked pensive momentarily and then said, "Chile Charlie, that's a fascinating question you asked. My response is based on Kingston's lack of resources to promote its fantastic tourist opportunities. So, we must get the word out through social media, the New Mexico Department of Tourism, and people like you who can tell our story effectively.

"As you know, the Southwest corner of New Mexico speaks to the imagination of the early days of the great history and rich culture. It contributes to our flavor of travel experience. We have a semiarid, subtropical climate with little precipitation, abundant sunshine, and low relative humidity.

"In Kingston, we need the infusion of hotels and restaurants and good signage to drive people here. It is a costly endeavor; we will not arrive at a level with a busload of tourists coming to our community. That is too bad because we have history and culture to give a valuable experience."

"Thanks for the information and everything that you have given me. I'll be in contact in two weeks," Chile Charlie said. He got into his El

Camino and whisked his way back to Camp Hope in Las Cruces.

CHAPTER TWENTY

CHILE CHARLIE LEARNS ABOUT CHIZ, NEW MEXICO

Chile Charlie was aroused from his usual mid-day siesta by a man dressed in a rancher's attire. "I'm looking for Chile Charlie," the stranger announced.

"You have found him," said Chile Charlie. "What can I do for you?"

The stranger introduced himself, "I'm Mario Trujillo. "I understand that you are gathering information about some of the ghost towns in New Mexico. Is that right?"

"Why, yes, I am Charlie answered with a worried look. "What does that have to do with me, Mario?"

"Well, Charlie, I have a story that will fascinate you, and you can use it in one of your presentations. Would you like to hear my story?"

"Yes, I would," Chile Charlie said. "Pull up a chair and talk to me. Please give me the background that you think I would need.

"Chiz may be the most exciting ghost town in New Mexico. Today, its population is only one person.

"Chiz was established in the mid-1800s and named after the Apache leader Cochise. His Apache name was "Chise" or "Cheis," meaning "wood." But that is not the story I want to tell you. The real story is about the comings and goings of my Trujillo family's early heritage.

"Here is the story.

"Chester Truillo was a blameless and upright man who feared God and turned away from evil. He had three sons and four daughters. His processions were one cow, a team of spavined (lamed) mules, one Razorback hog, and eight mongrel home pups. So, you see, this man was about as well off as most everybody else in Sierra County in those days.

"There came a day when the Sons of God came to present themselves before the Lord. Satan was also among them. And the Lord said unto Satan, "Whence, thou?"

Satan answered, "I've been going back and forth on the earth, and from walking up and down, it is looking for a man to join me.

"And the Lord said unto Satan, "Has thou considered my servant Trujillo? There is none like him on earth, a blameless, upright man who fears God and evil?

Satan answered the Lord. "Does Trujillo fear God for naught? Hast thou not made a hedge about him and his house and all he hath on every side?

Thou hast blessed the work of his hands, and the substance is increased in the land. But put forth by hand now and touch all he has, and he will curse thee to Thy face."

"There was no hedge, only a single strand of barbed wire about all Chester Trujillo had. The devil was right, though, in saying that the Lord had blessed the work of Trujillo. This year, his substance had increased in the land. There was a bumper cotton crop. Trujillo had harvested five bales. It was the reverse of what counted on when the crop was good. And the price was staying up. The price was rising by the day. Instead of selling when his crop was harvested, Trujillo put his bales in storage. He borrowed to live and waited for the best moment to sell.

"At this rate, he might pay something on the mortgage principal his old daddy had left as Trujillo's legacy. And fifteen or twenty years, he would own a piece of paper giving him soul and undisputed right, so long as he paid the taxes and broke his back plowing those fifty acres.

"Then the Lord said unto Satan, Behold, all that he hath is in your power. Do not put forth thy hand on him; he is mine." Satan went forth out of the presence of the Lord.

"Well," said Chester Trujillo, "When those five fat bales he had harvested stood in the shed running up a storage bill until he could not give the cotton away then.

"But instead of things getting better, times got worse. Times were so bad that a new and more extended word was needed: they were in the depression. Cotton that a man had plowed, seeded, chopped, picked, and harvested was going at a price to make your head shrink.

"The grocer whom Chester had had credit for twenty-four years picked this time to announce that he would have to pay cash. And would he please settle his Bill within the next thirty days? He hated to ask it, but they say we are in a depression." "Am I in it too?" asked Trujillo. What was the world coming to when cotton wasn't worth anything to anybody?

"For when he made his annual spring trip to the bank's loan department and was told that not only could they not advance them anything more but that his outstanding note was due.

"Nevertheless, when the ground was dry enough that you could pull your foot out of it, Trujillo plowed and planted more cotton again. What else was a man to do?

"There had been many times when Trujillo thanked God for taking his wife's uterus after the birth of their last girl. He thanked the Lord for his big family. There was a range of just six years among them; one brace of twins was included in the number to help around the farm. The boys were plow-broken, and the girls worked in the kitchen and around the house. And when cotton chopping time came, they all knew how to wield a hoe and pick cotton.

"One day the following spring, an Angel fell from heaven in the county agricultural agent. The agent told Chester that the government was ready to pay him, pay him, not to grow anything on twenty-five of his fifty acres. Trujillo asked, "What's the catch?

"No catch. It was a new law outside of Washington. He didn't need to be told that cotton prices were down. To raise them, the government was taking this step to lower production. The old law of supply and demand was in play. They would pay him as much not to grow anything on half his land as he would have made off the cotton. It sounded too good to be true. Something for nothing? From the government? And if true, something about it sounded a trifle shady and underhanded. Besides, what would you do?

"What is the world coming to? Hmm. I reckon my land, and I could both use a little rest. But taking money without working for it is not right? That sounds a bit fishy to me. My daddy would turn over in his grave.

"And if this is what voting straight Democrat for your whole life gets you, then next time around, I'll go, Republican, though God should strike me dead in my tracks at the polling booth.

"A man can only take so much squatting on the corner on Saturday afternoon without a nickel for a sack of Bull Durham or a matchstick of his own to chew on, Trujillo said to his friends.

"What's it all for?" Will somebody please tell me? What have I done to deserve this? I worked hard all my life. I've always paid my bills. I never diced, gambled, drank, or chased after women. I've always honored my old mom and daddy. I have done my best to provide for my wife and family. And I've tried to bring my children up decent and God-fearing. I've gone to church regularly. I've kept my nose out of other folk's affairs and minded my business. I've never knowingly done another man's dirt. Whenever the hat was passed around to help some poor woman left as a widow with orphaned children, I gave what I could. And what must I show for it? Look at me! Look at their hands. I take my punishment like a grown-up but never knowingly step out of line. So, what's it all for? Can any of you tell me? I'd be incredibly grateful to you if you would.

"Hellfire, we're all in the same boat said his neighbor. What good does it do to bellyache?

"Then, as luck would have it, a new and wonderful life came to the Trujillo family. While plowing, his plow struck something hard, stopping his two mules in place. He picked up the rock and threw it away when he thought it was special. He would take it to the local agricultural agent to determine what it was all about.

"The agent looked at the rock and said to Mr. Trujillo, "You're going to be rich. What you have found is gold.

"From poverty to riches caused problems within the close-knit family overnight. The girls clambered to leave the old homestead and move into town; they wanted to live in the most prominent house.

"Chester bought the Venderble House. He described the house: "You could have pastured a cow in the front lawn, which was so big. The grass was so thick you could walk on tiptoes for fear of muddying it with your feet. On the lawn were a life-sized cast-iron stag, silver balls on concrete pedestals, a croquet court, and a goldfish pond with a water fountain. You would wear a lead pencil

188

down to nothing to tally all the windows. The turrets, towers, cupolas, rounds, squares, and turnip-shaped roses are here and everywhere; the homestead looks like a town. You wanted to go around to the back door with your hat in hand. It takes a while to remember that it was yours.

?Chester wanted to have a housewarming so bad he could not stop listing those he would invite. The list was several pages long. His daughters created their list. The daughters sent out printed invitations, but Chester stood on the street corner and gave his invitations by word of mouth.

"Few people from either list showed up. First to arrive were their kin from the country, pickup trucks or mule-driven wagons and alive with kids. The men in suits smelled of mothballs, red in the face from their starched, buttoned, tieless collars, wetted-down hair drying and springing up like horses' manes, all crippled by pointed shoes, licking the cigar which Trujillo passed out. The women in dresses printed in jungle flowers, their hair in tight waves against their skulls. The kids were sliding down banisters, tearing through the halls, and skating across the wax parquet floors, trying to catch and goose one another.

"After the kinfolks arrived, a few of the many old friends and acquaintances Chester had invited came. Then arrived the others, those who knew better than to bring their children, some with colored maids at home to mind kids when the folks stepped out, people whom Chester had always tipped his hat to, little dreaming he would one day have them in his house. Some were owners of the land on which his kin sharecropped. Like cream from milk, the two groups are divided. He and his group found the kitchen and the backyard, leaving the girls and those they invited to the parlor and the front porch.

"Then, through the mist of the pride and pleasure of seeing all those town folks under his roof, Chester saw what was happening. All were laughing up their sleeves at what they saw, passing remarks about his girls, who would take their part against him if he tried to tell them they were being made fun of by their newfound friends. Poor things.

"Now his wife forgot about the Negro maid and served the guests herself. She was passing around the teacakes and the muffins. Her girls gave her a scoring look for doing the maid's job. So, the housewarming day went. People left as fast as they came. Most were snickering and laughing as they left. People found excuses for declining future invitations.

"Chester Trujillo was God-fearing, but his prosperity never fit his overalls well. He continued to wake up at four in the morning and could not get back to sleep. The habit of a lifetime is not quickly broken. But he could live there smiling, thinking he did not have to get up. No cow was waiting for him to milk, no mule harnessed, no feel to be plowed or pick of its cotton. Except, once awake, Chester saw no point in not getting up. It bored him to lie in bed doing nothing. Also, it was sinful.

"Chester did not want to waste a moment of his leisure. All day, each day was his now, to spend as you please according to his whim. Mere loafing was no pleasure to Chester; he had to be doing something. The men he used to find on the street were no longer there; they were all working. A lifetime of doing the same had left Chester feeling it was wicked and immoral of him to be there and not working.

"And so, the Lord blessed the latter end of Chester more than his beginning. For besides his gold mine, he never trusted gold that much. As an old country boy, he converted much of his gold into livestock: 14,000 head of white face cattle and five thousand Chinese hogs. He also had three sons and four daughters now, and he gave them each equal inheritance. However, each believed the others had been favored over them.

"Chester's time was short-lived, long enough for him to witness the despair of his sons and daughters. Chester Trujillo died, being old before his time and having had his fill of days."

Mario Trujillo finally said, "Chile Charlie, " the story behind the beginning of Chiz, New Mexico. Now Chester's Great Great Great-grandson lives there in a doublewide trailer. He paints and cares for the St. Gregory Catholic Church."

Several generations of Trujillo can trace their origins to this place. This writer hopes that this story provides the history of Chiz, population one.

CHAPTER TWENTY-ONE

CATRON COUNTY, NEW MEXICO

One of the best-kept secrets in New Mexico

Chile Charlie drove to the Village of Reserve, the county seat for Catron County. The fresh mountain air invigorated his senses as he exited his El Camino. The chirping of the birds was heard all around him.

The population of the community is less than five hundred hearty souls. He looked for the County Courthouse. The new county building was a prefabricated unit. The original courthouse was destroyed by a forest fire, which frequently occurs in Catron County. The building was constructed in the middle sixties and had a pitched tin roof.

As Charlie entered the building, he asked for the county clerk's office. Mr. Cedric Clark introduced himself to Charlie, "My name is Cedric Clark, and I am the elected county clerk. I've been the county clerk for the last fifteen years."

Mr. Clark had the look of a Marlboro cowboy. He was tall and raw-boned. His face looked like it was chiseled in stone.

Chile Charlie said, " I am glad to meet you, and I was hoping you could tell me about your county's history, culture, and economics."

Cedric said in a Catron County drawl, "I think you may have come to the right place, Charlie. I've lived here all my life and know the history and culture. I know a great deal about the economic development activities in this county."

"Let's walk over to the coffee shop and sit down and talk about Catron County."

"Janet, please look after the customers. Chile Charlie and I will be at the coffee shop for the next hour." They left. It was quite an effort to keep up with Cedric's long steps, which were more than adequate for a cowboy.

Cedric offered the following introduction to Catron County's secret as they sat down and ordered their coffee. Said, "The secret is in a blend of crisp mountain air, clear mountain streams, rugged slopes, narrow canyons, lakes, forest, and an eclectic collection of interesting residents, and I repeat, interesting residents."

"Here's the short story about Catron County. Two soldiers stationed at Fort Tularosa, where Geronimo and his Apache followers were being held, saw the possibility of pastureland offered by the surrounding fields, valleys, and mountains. They built their first settlement in 1874 in the upper San Francisco Plaza and established a successful sheep ranch. Other pioneers followed.

"Catron is the largest county in New Mexico, with 6,929 square miles of changing topography. It is larger than several eastern states—Delaware, Maryland, Rhode Island, or Connecticut. The county is sparsely populated with 3,725 people residence."

"In the 1870s, homesteaders and cattlemen fiercely battled the Apache Indians to settle Catron

County. Today, livestock production is the leading industry," Cedric said. He paused to take a drink.

"Reserve is the largest town in the county and serves as the county seat. The Gila National Forest surrounds the town. It was formerly named Frisco, deriving that name from the San Francisco River that flows through the county. Locals talk about the upper, middle, and lower San Francisco, all little frontier settlements. Reserve is the hub of the cow industry.

"San Francisco Plaza is a village remembered for the famous gunfight that featured lawman Elfego Baca and a crowd of rowdy Cowboys. In October 1884, eighty Texan Cowboys came to rec havoc on Frisco's little sleepy Hispanic community. The nineteen-year-old Baca single-handedly subdued the Cowboys in a three-day shoot-out during which more than four thousand bullets were fired and changed the course of history. John Muir created an impressive sculpture, Elfego Baca Memorial, which can be seen on Main Street of Reserve."

Cedric sat back and took a sip of his steaming hot coffee. "How am I doing?"

You're doing fine. My head is spinning with pictures of what it must have been like back then, but what's it like today?"

"Greenwood is one of the larger unincorporated communities in Catron County. It was founded in 1878, and it has three hundred residents. The town is located near the San Francisco River and south of Reserve.

"A major attraction is the 'Catwalk.' In 1889, silver and gold were discovered in the Mogollon Mountains above White Water Canyon outside Glenwood."

What's a Catwalk, Cedric?"

"The Catwalk refers to the original plank-board walkway placed atop the steel pipe used to bring water to the ore processing plant. The steel pipe hugged the canyon walls. The original pipes were washed away, but the Civilian Conservation Corps rebuilt it, so it is now a tourist attraction. It has been designated as a National Recreation Trail."

Charlie asked, "With all the wilderness, is hunting prominent in the Count?"

Cedric answered, "Big game hunters favor the county after bears, mountain lions, and elk. It is estimated that over 12,000 elk inhabit the area, three times the number of people in Catron County.

"The county also continues to be attractive for exploration and prospecting. You'll find white, extensive pine forest interspersed with large meadows, access to long horseback trails, two remote high plateaus, and broad sweeping vistas.

"Another feature that brings people into our county is the ghost town of Mogollon. The town offers remnants of the mining community, a bed and breakfast, gift shops, and a museum. The road is steep and winding and often impassable in the winter."

Charlie thanked Cedric and left the coffee shop, his head spinning with all the information about this wonderland.

CHAPTER TWENTY-TWO
LUNA COUNTY, NEW MEXICO
Land of pure water and fast ducks

Chile Charlie drove into the parking lot of the Luna County Courthouse. The building was built in 1910 and has been used for county affairs.

Chile Charlie entered the office of the County Clerk. He asks if he could talk to Eduardo Garcia, the County Clerk.

"I am Eduardo Garcia. To whom am I speaking," he asked.

Chile Charlie replied with his name, and he continued by telling Eduardo he would like to learn something about the history, culture, and economic development of Luna County.

Mr. Garcia said, "I will give you the required information."

"Please follow me to my conference room."

Entering it, Charlie saw a long table and several swivel chairs. The room accommodated ten people.

Both men sat facing each other at the long end of the table. Mr. Garcia started his information-giving declaration, "Luna County, New Mexico borders the Mexican border. There are two cities in the County-- Deming and Columbus. Deming is the largest of the two communities and the county seat. Columbus is smaller and has many historical stories to tell.

"Columbus has a unique and colorful history. The village was first established in 1891 across the border from Palomas, Mexico. In 1902, when the El Paso/Santa Fe railroad line opened a station at Columbus, the residents moved themselves and their households three miles north.

"Of particular interest to visitors and serious historians is the Columbus Historic Museum. The Columbus historic goal walking tour explains several sites associated with the Pancho Villa Raid and Furlong State Park, which were the original campgrounds of Pershing's Camp Furlong. The area has long experienced a successful blend of cultures between the Anglo and Hispanic peoples. This tradition is seen in the architecture, the food, and the celebrations that are so popular in the area.

"A short drive of three miles will put you at the United States Mexican border, and you can enter, but remember, you must have a passport to get back into the United States.

"Deming and Luna County have bragging rights to mild weather and lots of sunshine for outdoor enthusiasts to enjoy a list of activities, including golf, hiking, rock hounding, and birding."

Mr. Garcia asked, "Are you interested in collecting rocks?"

"Why, yes, I am."

Eduardo continued, "Gem and mineral collectors already know about Rock Hound State Park, where visitors are encouraged to gather up to fifteen pounds of mineral specimens for their collection. The park offered a visitors' center, a wide range of camping, hiking, and birding activities, and a botanical garden with a labyrinth.

"Spring Canyon, a day-use area with excellent birding, is practically adjacent to Rock Hound State Park. Two other popular state parks include City of Rocks and Poncho Villa State Park.

"You can tour two of New Mexico's most extensive vineyards and premier wineries in Deming. Enjoy low-impact aerobics activities on the Spring Canyon State Park trail or a walking tour of the historic downtown district filled with galleries, antique shops, coffee shops, an impressive Museum, and friendly people.

"The Deming--Luna Mimbres Museum is sometimes known as the 'Smithsonian of the Southwest.' It has a tremendous collection of Mimbres pottery and some of the best World War II information and equipment collections.

"The Museum is located in a 1916 red-brick National Guard Armory building. The Museum has about 25,000 square feet of exhibition space. The visitors will find a Military Room, a Doll Room, and a Tack Room. The Museum houses a Mimbres Room that displays prehistoric Mimbreno pottery.

"St. Clair Winery has been a local landmark in Deming since 1984, drawing visitors nationwide. Located in the Mimbres Valley wine region, the winery renewed the winemaking history of years past. The St. Clair Winery traditions are preserved by the Lescomb family, carrying on their families' six generations of winemaking history. They found the climate attractive to winemaking because of the ideal climate and the fertile soil to grow best quality grapes."

Chile Charlie thanked Mr. Garcia for his time and all the information and departed for Grant County.

CHAPTER TWENTY-THREE
GRANT COUNTY, NEW MEXICO

Chile Charlie walked into the County Building for Grant County in Silver City. He asked to see the County Clerk. Receptionists call for Jennifer Tagett. A nice-looking lady told Chile Charlie, "I am Jennifer; how can I help you?"

Chile Charlie said, "I am creating a booklet that features counties that made up Old West Country. I want to know about the history, culture, and economic developments in each of the counties."

Jennifer said she could fill the request if Charlie would step into her conference room, and we would spend some time talking. Chile Charlie and Jennifer stepped into the conference room.

Jennifer talked about what made up Grant County by saying, "For a vacation, a weekend getaway, or a stopover while visiting in the Southwest, Grant County is one place you wouldn't want to miss. The summer climate is cool and comfortable. You will enjoy crisp, clean air, sunshine, and the four gentle seasons. Recently, Silver City was selected as one of the healthiest places to live and retire. You can explore the ancient cultures and see the collection of distinctive black and white pottery developed one thousand years ago by the Mimbres Indians who inhabited the area.

"In Grant County, you can visit the 3.3 million-acre national forest and wilderness areas and today's modern ranching and mining industries. Enjoy authentic Mexican food, play eighteen holes of golf, explore museums and galleries, or shop the day away for unique South Western art and souvenirs. There are many places to stay, including cabins, campgrounds, bed-and-breakfast inns, historic hotels, and modern motels. Choose any season. There is always a reason to come to Grant County.

"Silver City is the centerpiece for Grant County. Folks have lived and worked in this part of the Southwest for more than 1200 years. Our unique combination of climate, lifestyle, environment, and opportunities is drawing new visitors and residents from around the world.

"Silver City is placed in the top one percent of over 3000 communities our size or larger as a place to live. Our low-risk lifestyle is a way of living. It eliminates all health-destroying habits and replaces them with health-promoting habits. It is based primarily on climate, elevation, terrain, and lack of urban stress.

"Silver City is proud of its reputation as an outstanding community and is a great place to work, live, or retire. Those are just a few of the good things about Silver City."

"Well, Chile Charlie, with all that information, how do you like the sound of Grant County?

Charlie said, "What a wonderful place. Maybe I can spend more time here."

Jennifer continued by telling Chile Charlie that Sunset magazine, August 2016, "Silver City was the home base at one time for both Billy the Kid and Geronimo."

"Silver City now has a population of about 10,000, a university, an active art community, and access to more than 3,000,000 acres of natural forest. In other words, it has been discovered.

"In an article in the New York Times in January 2020, the real New Mexico experience is offered by the people who live in Silver City. We are perched at the edge of the Gila National Forest in the high desert wonderland of Ponderosa, deep gorges, and red rock maces; Silver City is a bit rough around the edges, but that's how the locals like it.

"Southwest Aviator Magazine stated, "Silver City is an undiscovered mountain hideaway in a land of enchantment. It is a civilized hideaway on the outskirts of the vast Gila wilderness. People should plan a time to visit. Otherwise, they will regret you didn't stay longer.

"The Arizona Star newspaper said that Silver City is a treasure.

"Searchers indicated that Silver City is an outstanding community and a top place to retire.

"Other communities in Grant County, New Mexico, include Bayard, Hurley, and Pinos Altos.

"Bayard is five miles from Silver City. It is situated east of the Continental Divide at approximately 5800 feet. Each year in September, Bayard hosts Fort Bayard Days. It is an exciting day for people of all ages who want to learn more about Fort Bayard and the settling of the West. Over twenty living history centers will be set up around the parade grounds. The flag ceremony will begin at 9 AM, and the Learning Center closes at 3 PM. There are old-fashioned games and crafts for visitors to try.

"Josephine Clifford is the mother of Fort Bayard. She gives guided tours along with Dr. Bushnell, who plays the role of the Fort's physician.

"There are lectures about Native American history and so much more for students and adults of all ages to enjoy."

"Fort Bayard was built in 1866 to house Buffalo soldiers of the Ninth Cavalry. In the officers' quarters is this statue of gold medalist Cpl. Graves saved his patrol from destruction at the hands of the Apache.

"Hurley is about ten miles south of Silver City and is the Gateway to the mining community of Grant County. The Santa Rita Copper Mine is on the back door of Hurley. This open-pit mine is one of the largest in the world. You can visit the mine on special days with advance notice.

"Nestled in the Gila National Forest on a sunny southern mountain slope is historic Pinos

Altos, which means tall pines in Spanish. The village is the headquarters for fun and adventure in Silver City. Pinos Altos was established in 1860 when three frustrated 49ers stopped to take a drink in Bear Creek and discovered gold. The Main Street of this charming old town is like an old Western movie set. Many buildings date to the 1800s and have been restored with original memorabilia".

Jennifer whispered in Charlie's ear, "You sure don't want to miss the Gila Cliff dwellings designated as a National Monument."

Jennifer said, "Mogollon people built their homes in five natural caves in the 1200s."

Then Jennifer changed the subject and exclaimed, "Soldiers in 1866 built houses with local stone and timbers to shelter ten to fifteen individuals at City of Rocks State Park. The huge boulders were used to make origin-formed caves and sensible shapes. The park has picnic and camping sites and a wonderful Southwest cactus garden.

"There are mine tours at the Santa Rita open-pit copper mine. Copper mining was done by Apache, Spaniards, Mexicans, and then Americans. The nearby mines yield zinc, gold, magnesium, and iron today.

"The Trail of The Mountain Spirits is a Scenic Byways. The byway takes you through the forest, the cliff dwellings, the Mimbres culture, the abandoned mines, and the Buffalo Soldier Monument at historic Fort Bayard.

"The landscape is vibrant year-round and turns to a beautiful light brown in the fall, making Grant County a photographer's dream destination. There are numerous places to hike, drive, and explore. On a clear day, you can see forever. To get the whole experience, roll down your windows and drive across the Black Range Mountains.

"The area is awash with rich history and stories worth sharing," Jeniffer concluded.

Chile Charlie thanked Jennifer for all the information and left the County Courthouse on his way to Sierra County.

CHAPTER TWENTY-FOUR
SIERRA COUNTY, NEW MEXICO
Home of Spaceport America

Chile Charlie parked his El Camino in front of the County Building in Truth or Consequences and walked to the County Clerk's office. He asked to see the person in charge. Delmer Bobbem said, "Here I am. What can I do for you?"

Chile Charlie asked, "How did this town get its strange name?"

Delmer explained, "The change of town's name from Hot Spring to Truth or Consequences is credited to Ralph Edwards, who hosted a radio quiz program on NBC Radio entitled "Truth or Consequences." In March 1950, Ralph promised to air this show from a town that would change its name to match the program's name.

"Thanks, Delmer, for that information. That was remarkably interesting. I came to Truth or Consequences to learn about this wonderful Sierra, New Mexico County. I'm writing a small booklet, and I want to know about the area's history, culture, and economics. Can you help do that?"

"Why yes, Chile Charlie, I can always talk about our great county. I can do a good job of being the official spokesman for the local Chamber of Commerce, I am sure."

"We can step into my private office and start our conversation. Just follow me, Chile Charlie."

Delmar led the way down the hallway, entered his private office, and offered Charlie a chair. Delmar started, "Sierra County is the home of New

Mexico's premier water sports destination, an established center of natural hot mineral and healing arts, and the Home of Spaceport America. Sierra County is sometimes known as "the oasis of the desert."

"The major population center for the county is Truth or Consequences, which had a name change from Hot Springs.

"Does a fishing excursion sound like fun? Or a round of golf followed by a massage or mineral springs bath, Charlie?

"Maybe you are a history buff who enjoys exploring museums or old mines. Our downtown storefronts have become art galleries, boutiques, and secondhand stores. Many visitors like to visit the Geronimo Springs Museum and Geronimo Trails Visitors Center. You will find items from prehistoric times to present-day displays: fossils, Native American and Hispanic heritage, ranching, mining, and the name change from Hot Spring to Truth or Consequences.

"The city is surrounded by some of the state's best adventure sports opportunities and historic mining communities. Truth or Consequences sits atop some hot springs that generously feed the local bathhouses and spas. A complete range of massage and healing art treatments are always available.

"Known as America's most affordable town, Truth or Consequences and Elephant Butte Lake has long been a destination for those seeking to rejuvenate their spirits in its hot mineral waters.

"Elephant Butte Lake State Park has the second largest lake in New Mexico. There are boat ramps, campsites, RV sites, fishing, hiking, and birdwatching.

"The Rio Grande River runs through Truth or Consequences. Therefore, the state park campsites offer fishing, kayaking, and tubing. The nearby Ralph Edwards Park also has all the services.

"There are several Old West towns outside the city limits of Truth or Consequences. They include Hillsboro and Kingston, which hold memories of miners and gunfighters, the Black Range Museum, churches, and gift shops. Geronimo Trail Scenic Byways and Cuchillo Interpretive Center are good places to visit.

"The terrain varies from desert to mountain forest. Cuchillo has a museum and pecan groves.

"The spot in the road Lake Valley is part of the Backcountry Byway. This scenic byway goes from Lake Valley, north through Hillsboro, and ends at Truth or Consequences.

"Monticello/Placita was settled in 1856 by ranchers and farmers. They called it the "Canyon of the Cottonwoods. Chloride is a small town with a Pioneer Museum that everyone says is first class."

Chile Charlie extended his gratitude to Delmer, appreciating the wealth of information he received. With a courteous nod and a warm handshake, he bid farewell to his host, embarking on the journey back to his sweet home — Las Cruces.

THE END

As Charlie navigated the familiar streets, memories of his travels through places and events in New Mexico played like a vivid movie reel. The sun dipped below the horizon, glowing warmly on the picturesque landscapes surrounding him. The air was filled with a sense of accomplishment and newfound knowledge.

Chile Charlie reflected on the significance of the information he acquired with each step. It was a crucial puzzle piece in his ongoing quest to know the great state of New Mexico. As he approached his residence, he couldn't help but feel a mix of anticipation for new adventures.

Suddenly into his favorite chair, Charlie took a moment to process the month's revelations. He reached for a notepad, jotting down key points and formulating an action plan. The journey to learn more about the great state of New Mexico was far from over, and Las Cruces was both a haven and a launching pad for the challenges ahead.

Tomorrow held new possibilities, and with a renewed sense of purpose, he prepared for the next chapter in his quest for stories to be told about the history, culture, and economics of New Mexico.

Author's Notes

Readers who enjoy learning about mysteries' interworking behind an author's style will find my bibliography on my website, www.georgepintarbooks.com.

Some of my writings summarize my professional career as a business leader. *Digging Deeper into Networking and Build Strong Communities Using Community Education* are self-published. You can purchase them on Amazon.com.

The authorship of my fictional character Chile Charlie includes *Revisit Musings of an Ostrich Farmer, Chile Charlie's View of Old West Country, A New Peek at Old West Country, The Adventures of Chile Charlie, A Cloud-eater Saga,* and *Never Too Late?* Readers can purchase these books at www.Amazon.com.

Here is how you can reach me:

George Pintar

853 Chile Court

Las Cruces, NM 88001

575-680-6515

Made in the USA
Columbia, SC
23 July 2024

38601501R00126